THE RULE BREAKER

CATHRYN FOX

COPYRIGHT

ISBN Print: 978-1-989374-28-3

ISBN ebook: 978-1-989374-29-0

LIAM

As we head up the stairs to the Big Brothers Big Sisters of America organization, I tilt my head and grin as my gaze rakes over the Seattle Shooter's newest publicist—probably hired just for me. Probably? Oh hell, who am I kidding. He was most definitely hired for me. I am, after all, known as the rule breaker.

"What?" Jeremy asks, like he can feel my eyes on him as we walk. As the late June sun shines down on us, he reaches for the door with barrel arms, and I lift my head to take in his questioning eyes. At six-foot, two hundred pounds, I consider myself a big guy, but Jeremy still towers over me and those muscles don't come from a gym or a rink, like mine. He grew up on a farm and I'm guessing those arms come from picking up tractors or something. He doesn't fit the image I envisioned for a publicist. Maybe that's sexist on my part, or maybe I'm influenced by all the chick flicks I've watched.

I chuckle. "You know, in every makeover movie I've ever watched, the publicist is always a hot woman who ends up falling in love with the guy she's 'fixing.'" I stop to do air quotes around the word fixing. Is this trip to the Big Brothers organization about fixing me, changing my image? Damn right it is. That's what too many fights will get you, especially when they're off the ice, videoed by every patron at the bar and splashed all over social media.

"You watch a lot of romantic comedies, do you?" he asks with a smirk.

I shrug. "Three older sisters. I couldn't escape it." I'm not about to tell him I enjoyed those chick flicks just as much, and maybe even more, than my siblings. No, if I admitted that, I'd have to cash in my man card, and that just can't happen. The world can't know I'm quiet and introverted, and my antics on the ice and at the bars are for show only. The world expects rowdy from me, so I give them rowdy. It's all about keeping the fans happy, right?

Although I'm not too sure anyone was happy with that leaked sex tape a puck bunny I slept with sold to Dirt, an online tabloid that breaks the biggest stories in celebrity and entertainment news. I guess she wasn't happy that I didn't want a long-term relationship, and really, she knew that from the start anyway. It's not a secret that I don't do commitment, the secret is *why* I don't.

"Should I be worried about you falling for me?" he asks. I laugh at that and he adds, "Just so you know, I like you, but I don't swing that way."

His heavy hand lands on my shoulder, as I walk through the open door and laugh out loud. "Ditto." Everyone knows I'm a man-whore. It's all part of my image, and another reason I'm staring at a big desk, the beige walls behind the receptionist splattered with posters of smiling kids doing fun activities with their mentors. Honestly, how anyone thinks I'm capable or qualified to guide a youth is beyond me.

I was the youngest of four, with little responsibility at home. Not only do my fans call me the rule breaker, I live up to it. That's not the kind of guy who toes the line and sets good examples. But if I want to keep my coach happy, and keep my endorsements, mentoring a youth and cleaning up my image is what I must do. But what will the fans think? Are they going to drop me because I'm not who they think I am, not living up to their rough and tough expectations? Talk about a rock and a hard place. Nevertheless, I have a seven-figure endorsement contract that I don't want to lose, and I damn well hope I don't lose my fans once I become the poster boy for good sportsmanship.

The middle-aged lady behind the counter smiles up at me, and I glance at her nametag. "Liam Dalton," she says and stands, her hands going to her round cheeks. "It's so nice to meet you. I'm a huge fan."

"Thanks," I say and tug on my ballcap. "If you'd like, you can grab your phone and we can get a selfie."

Her eyes go wide. "Really? You wouldn't mind?" She glances around. "I mean, we're not supposed to harass our volunteers, especially the famous ones."

"But I asked you, Rita," I tell her with a smile. "And I'd be nothing without fans like you." I wave my hand. "Get on over here."

She snatches up her phone, comes out from around the desk, and holds it out, but can't quite angle it right. I take it from her to get a better reach and put my arm around her shoulder. She's practically vibrating with excitement as I snap the picture. "There you go."

Beside me, Jeremy smiles and gives a nod, approving my behavior. I'm not putting on an act here. I love my fans and take all the time in the world for them. She shuffles back to her chair, and her face is glowing as she hands over a pen and clipboard.

"If you could just fill these out. Mr. Sanders will be with you in a moment. You can have a seat over there."

As I walk toward the small waiting room, toys in one corner, muffled voices reach my ears. I drop down into a plastic chair, and spot a young boy staring at me. He's tugging on his mother's dress with one hand and pointing to me with another.

"That's him, that's Liam Dalton," the boy says repeatedly. I'm not great with ages—heck I can never remember my nieces' and nephews' birthdays—but I'd say he's around four or five.

Looking a little frazzled and rushed, his mother drops to her knees and says something to her son, something quiet and private—something that sounds like she doesn't want to bother me, and that they're in a big hurry—but her little boy is so excited, I don't think he's listening. My gaze drops to take in her perfect, heart-shaped backside as she aims it my way. I should look away. I want to look away. Damned if I can help myself, though. You didn't miss the part where I said I was a man-whore, right?

I quickly pull myself together and cleanse my wayward thoughts. She's here with her son for Christ's sake, not to get ogled by me, and I shouldn't be taking pleasure in the way her dress hugs her curves. I'm about to stand and ask if they'd like a picture, when the mom turns to me, a wobbly, apologetic smile on her face.

"I'm sorry to bother you," she says, and stands, sweeping her hand down a summery blue dress, the fabric splattered with big, white daisies. My gaze tracks the motion of her hands, going lower and lower until I reach long slender calves. Sexy and adorable. There's a combination I don't see every day. "My son Gavin would like to say hello, if that's okay?"

"Of course, it's okay," I say and jump up, but my fast reaction seems to startle her. She stumbles back a bit, and my stomach clenches at her skittish reaction. Shit, I know I'm a big guy, and can be overbearing, but I didn't mean to scare her. I slow my pace, and when I reach the child, I go down on one knee, facing her son at eye level.

"Do you watch hockey, Gavin?"

He nods emphatically and I smile at him. "I watch it with Holden. Mom doesn't like it."

His mom's face is twisted, apologetic once again when I glance up. "That's okay, not everyone likes hockey." I resist the urge to ask him if Holden is his father. Then again, he would have called him Dad, right, and am I really thinking about hitting on this woman as she stands here with her child? Jesus, fuck, I am. Now that we've all established that I'm a grade-A asshole, I ask, "What's your favorite team?"

"Seattle Shooters," he says and makes a motion like he's taking a shot.

I laugh at that. "Atta boy," I say and ruffle his hair. "Who's your favorite player?"

"Cole Cannon," he answers without missing a beat.

His mother sucks in a tight breath. "Sorry," she says, but I laugh it off.

"Don't be sorry." I glance up at her, take in her big blue eyes and the way she's wrestling her hair back into a big clip. Dog hair clings to her dress, at least I think it's dog hair, and with a face free of makeup, her blonde hair all over the place, nothing about the woman screams composed or poised, which somehow intrigues me all the more. Strange, I know. But Jesus, she's absolutely gorgeous. I tear my gaze away, despite the fact that I'd like to take all the time in the world to admire her, figure out why she's so agitated, and focus in on her son. "I wouldn't want anything but honesty from you, Gavin." I take my hat off and put it on his head. "A little big, but it's yours if you'd like it."

He takes it off, looks at the Shooters emblem, and turns to his mother. "Mommy, can I have it, please?"

"I don't think we should take it," she says, and I'm not sure what it is, but my stomach tightens again, that strange protective feeling I had earlier once again careening through my blood as I note the uncertainty in her eyes. "He's not supposed to take things from strangers," she clarifies.

"Oh, sorry. I never thought of that." I smile at Gavin. "How about this." I hold my hand out for a shake and he puts his small palm in mine. "I'm Liam Dalton, and you are..."

"Gavin Peterson."

"Well, Gavin, now that we're friends, would you like my hat?"

He nods and his mother lets loose a small laugh that curls around me. I lift my head to find her smiling. "Thanks," she says. "I'm sure he'll never take it off."

Gavin puts his hat back on. "Are you here to get a big brother too?" he asks, and my heart squeezes a bit.

"No, but I'm here to be a big brother."

Blue eyes go wide as he stares up at me. "Can you be my big brother?"

"Gavin," his mom says quickly. "We can't ask things like that, and I'm sure Liam's already been matched."

Gavin's shoulders sag a little, and I cast a quick glance toward the receptionist. "Have I been matched?" I ask.

"Not yet. We haven't even received your paperwork yet." The phone rings, and Rita answers it with a happy chirp in her voice.

"I guess there's still a chance." I stand and hold my hand out to Gavin's mom. "I'm Liam Dalton."

She puts her hand in mine, and I catch her sweet scent that reminds me of the citrusy jellybeans I used to eat as a kid. Damned if that's not another thing that attracts me to her.

"I know who you are," she says.

I angle my head. "Oh really, and here I thought you didn't watch hockey?"

"No, but I do read the papers."

I inwardly cringe. "You know you can't believe everything you read, right?"

She hikes her big purse up higher. It looks like it weighs a ton. "You didn't punch that guy out at Nelly's bar last week?"

I shrug my shoulders, and kick at an imaginary rock on the floor. "Well yeah, but he was messing with a girl who didn't want to be messed with, so what was I supposed to do?"

"Oh, so you were defending some girl's honor, were you?" she says, her lips twitching as she holds back a smile.

"Darn right, I was," I say, watching my language in front of Gavin.

Gavin grabs his mom's dress again. "Mommy, can Liam be my big brother?"

She opens her purse—which could double as a suitcase—checks the time on her phone, and says, "Gavin, why don't you go play for a quick second?"

Gavin scrunches up his nose, and skips away to the play area. "I didn't get your name," I say.

"It's Harper," she says in a low voice, and then adds, "Liam, I don't know how to say this. I don't really know you and I don't want to hurt your feelings, but I don't think you'd be a good match for my son."

I shove my hands into my jeans. "Yeah, it's okay. No worries." I'm not sure why, but my stomach is tight, like I'd just taken a stick to the gut. With my reputation, did I really expect this woman to trust that I'd be a good role model for her son? But there's something else. Something I can't quite put my finger on, something that makes me want to tuck her under my arm and protect her from a world that might have been cruel to her and her son.

She checks the time again. "I do have to go."

I back up a bit. "Okay."

"Gavin, come on. We need to get home."

Gavin's eyes are hopeful as he comes racing over. "Is Liam going to be my big brother?" he asks. Harper opens her mouth, and then closes it again. She doesn't want to disappoint Gavin, that much is certain.

"No, I don't think...I just...chances of you guys matching..."

Gavin's smile falls, and my heart sits heavy for the kid. "Gavin," I begin, coming to her rescue. "I think they might have already matched you, and you know what, I bet your big brother is going to be the best big brother in the world." I glance at Harper. "Can I have your phone?" She eyes me with uncertainty, and I laugh. "Don't worry, I'm not putting my digits in your contacts. I'm a lot of things, but I'm not a creep. I just want to get a picture with Gavin."

"Right." She hands me the phone, and I drop down next to Gavin. He puts his arm around my shoulder as I take a bunch of pictures. "Now you can show Holden."

"Mommy, Holden won't believe this!"

"Pics or it didn't happen," I say, and when he stands there staring at me, I laugh. Of course, he doesn't know what I mean. He's a kid with no social media presence. "Am I Holden's favorite?" I ask.

"No, he likes Alec. He wants to be a goalie like him."

"Am I anyone's favorite?" I ask with a laugh as I stand back up. Gavin looks through the pictures as I nod to his mom. "Nice meeting you, Harper."

She stands there staring at me, and I can almost hear the wheels spinning. What is going through that pretty head of hers?

A big strand of blonde hair falls from the clip, and I resist the urge to brush it from her face. She blows it away and says, "You're really good with him. Do you...have kids?"

"No, but I like kids," I say quietly, thinking of my nieces and nephews. "That's why I'm here." It's not a lie, I do like kids, and when I was told to clean up my image and do volunteer work, I was the one who chose this organization.

"I've seen pictures of you and other teammates at the children's hospital. That's a really nice thing that you guys do."

"Mommy, look at this one," Gavin says, and holds the phone up. She smiles as she takes a look.

"That's a great picture," she says, and puts her hand on his hat. Her gaze lifts, focuses back on me. "I mean, I'm sorry...I just..."

I hold my hands up, palms out. "It's okay," I say. "I'm sure he'll be matched with someone great." The front door opens, and in walks a woman and a little girl. The girl heads straight for the play area, and I glance at Jeremy as he scrolls through his phone. "I'd better get those forms filled out."

"Okay," she says, and takes Gavin's hand. "It was nice meeting you, Liam." I go back to my chair, disappointment sitting heavy and I'm not sure I really understand it. Then again, maybe it's because I always get what I want, and this woman shut me down at hello. I smile, liking her all the more.

Harper steps up to the reception desk and speaks quietly. A moment later, she disappears through the door, and something in my gut tells me to get my ass in gear and go after her. Not just because she's the sweet kind of girl that I should be photographed with, or that she doesn't like hockey and clearly doesn't like me—something I'd like to change—but because, like her son, she needs someone rock-solid in her life. But thanks to my reputation, that guy will never be me.

HARPER

"Okay, that's it, you're certifiable."

Sitting at my kitchen table, I stare at my best friend as she flips through the photos on my phone. Her jaw is practically sitting on the table, as she shakes her head at me, unable to wrap her brain around me turning down Liam's offer. Then again, did he really offer to be Gavin's big brother? He only said there was a chance. "Harper, what the hell is wrong with you?"

"How much time do you have?" I tease, even though Emma knows everything about me, everything from how Gavin's father took off after he was born, never to be heard from again, to the next guy in my life who slowly drained the inheritance Mom and Dad left to me in their will four years ago, when Gavin was only one. Simply put, I'm a bad judge of character.

Emma continues to stare at the pictures, and I'm about to offer her a napkin to wipe the drool from the corners of her mouth when she drops my phone and shakes her head. "You said no to Liam. Girl, he could have been Gavin's big brother, and your big daddy."

I pick up my mug and cover my smile with it. Maybe I shouldn't have told her every single word we exchanged, and maybe I shouldn't like talking or thinking about him so much. "That's not funny."

"Then why are you laughing?"

So much for hiding my reaction. I can't get anything by her. She glares at me, waiting for an answer. But I'm not about to tell her I'm smiling to hide what I'm really feeling deep inside me—right around the juncture of my legs. I took one look at Liam when he dropped to his knees in front of my son, and nearly sank down with him. I mean, I've seen the pictures, know he's smoking hot. But the photos of him splashed in the tabloids pale in comparison to the real thing. Liam Dalton is seriously the hottest guy on the face of the earth, and when he smiled at me, I swore I could hear the clench of my ovaries.

Emma snickers. "He was that hot, huh?"

"What?" I ask. "Wait, why are you staring at me like that?" Once I realize my coffee cup has been hovering over my mouth as my mind drifted, I take a big sip.

"Because you totally zoned out, and I'm guessing that's because you were thinking about big daddy and all the spankings he could give you. I mean, you did see the leaked sex tape, didn't you?"

I laugh, and coffee comes out my nose, which stings horribly. "Ohmigod." I jump up and run to the small bathroom just off the kitchen. Emma's laughter fills my small house, rising over the sounds of Gavin and Holden playing video games in the living room as I grab a cloth and wipe my face.

"No, I did not see the tape, nor do I want to see the tape," I call out. "And that hurt."

"I bet he'd make it hurt so good."

"Are you still at it?" I step back into the kitchen, and find her on my phone again.

"Man, I need to have a kid." She glances up at me, the hope in her eyes reminding me of the look Gavin gave me before I sort of shot down his dream of having Liam as a big brother. Did I make the right decision? "Do you think he'll still be offering his big daddy services in nine months, 'cause girl-friend, I'd like to match my face right to his—"

"Stop." I grab the phone from her and set it aside. "I'm sure we're not going to be matched, and I don't want Gavin with a guy like Liam, anyway."

"You mean a guy who fights to defend a woman's honor. A guy who was nice to Gavin, gave him a hat and took pictures with him." She puckers her lips. "Yeah, I see what you mean."

"I just...have to be careful who I bring into Gavin's life, Emma."

She touches my hand. "Is this really about Gavin?" she asks.

I stiffen. "What's that supposed to mean?" I ask, even though I already know the answer and she knows I know it.

"It took me forever to convince you to get Gavin a big brother in the first place."

"He needs the male influence, you were right."

"But what do you need, Harper?"

"I don't need—"

"That's where you're wrong. You're twenty-eight years old with lots of needs that are going neglected as you let life pass before your eyes." I'm about to tell her I'm a busy single parent, working full time and trying to save for my own pet store and doggy daycare business, when she holds her hand up to stop me, the look on her face suggesting she's heard it all before. "Look, all I'm saying is you shut down." She puts her hand over her heart. "In here. You don't go out, don't date, don't do anything just for you."

"What does any of this have to do with Liam being Gavin's big brother?"

"Because you were attracted to him, and that frightens you. I think he'd be good for Gavin." She wags her brow. "And for you."

"Are you suggesting—"

"I'm suggesting you have some fun. He has a reputation, I know, so you know he's not looking to put a ring on it. Why not have some fun with him, and Gavin gets a superstar, professional hockey player for a big brother?"

I shrug. "I doubt they'll be matched, and it could take months. That's what we were told anyway." My cell phone rings, and I practically jump out of my chair. I reach for it and see that it's from the Big Brothers Big Sisters organization. I slide my finger across the screen.

"Hello."

"Harper, we have good news." I instantly recognize the receptionist's voice. I cover the phone and tell Emma it's Rita.

"You have a match?"

"We do. How would you like to bring Gavin in tomorrow to meet with him?" Her voice is full of sing-song excitement.

I consider my schedule for tomorrow. I work at the pet store in the morning, and then have to walk a few dogs in the afternoon. "Would three o'clock be okay?"

"Perfect, see you then."

I end the call and glance at Emma. "They found him a match. That was crazy fast."

She puts her hands on the table and stands. "I'll keep my fingers crossed that it's Liam. But not my legs. Jared is coming over later, and I believe I'll be thinking about hot daddy when I take him to my bed."

"How are we even friends?" I ask with a laugh. Honestly though, Emma is the best friend a girl could have, and she gives good advice. Should I take it where Liam is concerned? Should I see about matching him with my child?

See about matching him with me?

Wait, what! I am not going to get emotionally tangled with the guy who's going to mentor my son. That would be wrong on so many levels. But what about a quick hook-up? Sex only, no emotions. Would that be wrong?

Yes, it would!

Then again, all this is moot. They just called to say they had a match, and Liam is just getting processed in the system. It could never happen that fast. Right? Unless, he's already been cleared. He does, after all, spend time with kids in the children's hospital. I'm sure he's already had every criminal background check they needed.

"You just keep thinking about what I said, Harper."

I blink my mind back into focus and find Emma staring at me with a knowing look on her pretty face. "Goodbye, Emma," I say and point to the door as she laughs.

"Later, babe," she says.

Once she's gone, I head in to check on the boys. "Mommy, can Holden stay for dinner?" Gavin asks.

My heart pounds harder in my chest as I look at my sweet boy and his best friend. "If it's okay with his mom?"

"It is," Holden says barely sparing me a glance as he maneuvers the game controller and I just laugh.

"I'll check in with her." I step back into the kitchen, and call Violet. Emma, Violet and I go way back to junior high, and while we're all so different—Violet is married and has Holden, Emma has no desire to settle down, and I'm a single mom—we've all remained friends. After Gavin and I left the Big Brothers organization, we stopped to pick Holden up. I honestly don't know what I'd do without Holden and his family in my life. With the amount of babysitting they do for me, it's the least I can do to have Holden for dinner.

Violet answers the phone with, "Is my tater tot giving you trouble?"

I laugh. "No trouble at all. Apparently, he has your permission to stay for dinner."

"That kid," she says with a laugh. "He's going to be the death of me when he becomes a teen."

"We both have eight more years before we have to worry about that." As soon as the words leave my mouth, my throat tightens. Honestly, all I ever do is worry about Gavin. By the time he reaches thirteen, I want him to be a respectful young man. I've been doing my best to be both Mom and Dad, but sometimes it's not easy. Sometimes? Okay, pretty much all the time. Emma was right about getting him a big brother. Was she right about me getting back out there, getting myself a big daddy?

Am I really considering this?

Oh God, I am.

"Sure, he can stay," Violet says, her voice pulling me back. "I'll come pick him up later."

"Sounds great." I'm about to end the call when she clears her throat, the way she always does when she's about to take center stage and climb on her soap box. "What's up?" I ask.

"Don't you have something to tell me?"

"Ah, nope." I can just visualize her standing there, tapping her manicured nails on the countertop. Her name might be Violet, and she's well kept, but she's no delicate flower. None of us are. I glance at my nails, chipped with half the paint peeled off. I am so not put together like my friends. But I'm a pet groomer, and walk dogs for a living. Someday though, I'll have my own pet store and grooming business. "Not that I can think of."

"Okay, that's it, *former* best friend," she says, and I'd be worried, but I hear the lightness in her tone. That's when I realize where she's going with this, and I groan. "Oh, yeah, I hear that groan, and if you knew what was good for you, you'd be making those same noises with Liam Dalton on top of you."

"I'm going to kill Emma."

"Did you really think she wouldn't tell me? And I'm mad that you didn't."

"It's nothing. It's no big deal. We ran into him. That's all that happened." Maybe that's not all that happened. I can't deny that I caught him checking me out. His gaze going from daisy to daisy on my dress, lingering over my breasts and legs. A warm shiver moves through me, and my traitorous nipples tighten, just like they did when he flashed me that panty-melting grin. God, no wonder women are all over him. He's the hottest guy I've ever set eyes on and I really hope he didn't notice my reaction to him.

"You should have said yes. He'd be an awesome big brother, and anything else you might need him for, and yes, I'm talking about your beaver canoe."

The fact that she's always called a woman's private parts their beaver canoe never fails to make me laugh.

"Are you sure you're not saying that because you and Jason want to meet him." Her husband Jason is a huge Seattle Shooters fan, and no doubt is going to lose his mind over this.

"You should have said yes," Jason screams out in the background.

Violet laughs. "That's three against one, girlfriend, and no, this isn't about us, it's about you and Gavin. You know we always have your best interests at heart, and well, if you're going to dust off the 'beaver-can't do' and turn it into a 'beaver-can do' why not do it with God's gift to women himself."

"Hey, I thought I was God's gift to women," Jason yells.

"You're God's gift to me, baby." My heart squeezes as I listen to them. That's what I want. Right there. Couples who tease, laugh and have fun together. I'd be lying if I said I wasn't envious. I'm just too damn afraid of getting hurt, of watching another man walk out of Gavin's life—out of mine. Although Devon didn't walk out. I kicked him out. Too bad I hadn't done it before he drank and gambled my inheritance away, getting physically abusive when I told him it was over. He walked out the door, taking my dreams of running my own business within the next couple of years right along with him. At least he didn't leave with my head.

"You know his reputation, right? Would he really be a good influence on Gavin?"

I want Gavin to grow up respecting women, not sleeping his way through the alphabet. As Violet tries to convince me that he's a player on and off the ice, but that doesn't mean he's not good with kids, and I could use a no-commitment 'beaver can-do' banging, my mind drifts. Liam might have been checking me out, and hell, I was checking him out too, but he seemed so different than he's portrayed in the papers. Then again, I'm not a good judge of character, right?

Violet sighs into the phone. "Just tell me you'll think about it."

"I'll think about it."

"Okay, I'll stop by after dinner to pick up my tater tot."

I end the call, and get to work on cooking, all the while trying to keep my mind off a guy who is suddenly living rent free in my head. I feed the boys, and after Violet picks Holden up, I give Gavin a bath and tuck him into his bed.

"Night, kiddo."

I'm about to turn the light off and shut his door when his soft, tired little voice stops me.

"Mommy."

"Yeah?"

"How come I don't have a daddy like Holden does?"

My heart squeezes in my too tight chest, and I take a gulping breath. Sooner or later, I knew he was going to ask the question. Perhaps being at the Big Brothers organization really brought it home for him. I hover at the door and look at Gavin's innocent face. After losing his grandparents at the young age of one, and having two men leave his life, he deserves stability, someone who's going to put him first. But I'm so goddamn scared to get back out there. Honestly, I'm not even sure there are any good guys left.

Redirecting the conversation, I say, "Well, you're going to get a big brother soon. That's pretty exciting, isn't it?"

He holds his hands up and crosses his fingers. "I really hope it's Liam."

"I know you do, kiddo."

"Maybe someday he could be my daddy."

I groan inwardly, and really wish I wasn't thinking about him being my 'big' daddy, too.

3

LIAM

I race up the steps to the Big Brothers organization and pull open the heavy door, anxious to meet the child I matched with. As soon as I enter the empty reception area, Harper's citrusy scent curls around me. Either it's my imagination, or she's back in the building with Gavin. I'm going with the former, considering I haven't been able to get her out of my head since meeting her, and yeah, maybe I did have a date with the palm twins last night. So what if I chose that over hitting the club and picking up a woman? I'm not supposed to be doing that anymore, yet I'm not one-hundred percent sure that's what kept me home last night.

"Hi Rita," I say, and she gives me a big smile. For a second I think about asking her for Harper's contact information, but like I said before, I'm not a creeper, and that somehow seems like I'd be crossing a line.

"Liam, so nice to see you again." She stands and waves me to follow. "Come on in and meet your little brother. We'll give you time to talk and play, and if you and the child's mother feel like it's a good fit, we go from there."

"Sure thing." I adjust my ballcap and follow her down the hall. She's all giddy when she opens the door and waves her hand for me to enter. I step through the door, take one look at the boy on the floor playing with the toy cars, and a wide smile spreads across my face. It dissolves just as quickly when I hear Harper's sharp intake of breath.

"Liam, are you my big brother?" Gavin asks, as he jumps to his feet, his big smile wrapping around my heart and squeezing.

"Ah..." I say and glance at Harper.

"My wish came true, Mommy. Last night I crossed both fingers and wished really hard."

"Gavin," I begin, not sure how I'm going to break the kid's heart, but Harper made it clear I wasn't the man for her son. "I don't think—"

"He doesn't think he could be happier," Harper says, interrupting me. My gaze flies to hers, and I take in her bunched forehead, the tightness in her lips.

"You're happy you got me?" Gavin asks, like he's not used to anyone wanting him, and it damn near breaks my heart.

Harper turns from me, and smiles as she talks to her son. "Of course, he is, Gavin. Getting you as a little brother is the best thing that could happen to anyone."

His smile lights up the room, and behind me Rita says, "Harper, let's talk in the other room while these two get to know each other."

"Can I talk to you in the hall for a second?" Harper asks.

"Sure. Be right back, kiddo," I say and tug on his too big Seattle Shooters ball cap. I step into the hall with Harper and Rita.

"Isn't this wonderful?" Rita says. "I was thrilled when they matched. I couldn't wait to see the look on Gavin's face."

"It is wonderful," Harper says. "Do you mind if I talk to Liam for a quick second?"

"Of course, dear. Meet me in that room when you're done."

She disappears and Harper leans against the wall, like her legs can no longer hold her up. Damned if I don't want to put my arm around her and give her the support she needs.

She shakes her head, a humorless smile on her face. "Well, this is quite the surprise."

"Harper, if you don't want—"

"Do you think I could say no to him?" She shakes her head. "I just...if you're going to do this, I need you to be there for him." She adjusts her big purse, and glances at the floor, like she's trying to choose her words carefully. "This is hard to explain."

"He's had loss. I get it." She's had loss too, it's written all over her, but I'm not about to bring that up.

"I don't want him to be waiting for you, to be counting on you, relying...and..." She takes a breath and lets it out slowly. "I don't want him to get hurt."

"I'm going to do the best I can, Harper. I've never been a big brother before. I can't promise I won't make mistakes. But once I give someone my word, I stick to it."

"The fighting, the drinking. I can't have another drinker in his life. I just...can't."

As the vision of her life, her loss, becomes clearer, I nod. She's right about me. I do drink too much. Partly because it helps me cope with my role of the Rule Breaker, and partly because it helps me be someone else—someone everyone likes.

"What about a hockey player who wants to help a kid out, and hopefully make a positive impact?" Christ, I sound like the poster boy already.

She gives me a small smile. "I'd like that very much."

She pushes off the wall and is about to leave, when I say, "I think this is going to be good for me too."

"That would be nice, Liam," she says her voice soft, her blue eyes the color of the sky the morning after a storm blew through.

She leaves and I keep my gaze on her, admire the summery dress she's wearing, which is once again full of animal hair. It makes me smile for some reason. At least she doesn't seem as rushed today as she was yesterday. Once she's inside with Rita, I open the door, and find Gavin back on the floor.

"Hey buddy, how are you?"

He jumps up. "Can we play outside?"

"I think we have to stay in here for a bit, but maybe we can later, if it's okay with your mom."

"She's okay with it," he informs me, and I laugh, giving a wink to the mirror, knowing Rita and Harper are on the other side, watching me. "How about we play with some of these cool cars while we wait for your Mom." I drop down onto my side, and grab a toy car, running it over the mat. It's funny because I had the same mat when I was Gavin's age. I wonder what other toys Mom still has up in the attic. I make a note to ask her.

"What's your favorite car?" I ask, as he drops down across from me, mimicking my position exactly, right down to the way I have my head braced on my hand. As I watch him reach for his favorite car—a very sporty corvette—it really occurs to me how much influence I'll have over this boy. Like I said before, I've never had to take on too much responsibility, but for the first time in my life, I'm looking forward to it.

"When I was in Miss Tammy's, we had show and tell."

"Did you now?" I ask, noting his change in subject, and having no idea who Miss Tammy is. "What did you bring?"

"I brought Charlie. I think he's Mommy's favorite, but she's not supposed to have favorites."

My brow furrows and I glance at the mirror again, having no idea who Charlie is and why he's Harpers favorite. Is it possible that she has 'uncles' coming and going all the time? Growing up, my buddy Beck had lots of uncles, most of them were nothing but abusive assholes. Jesus, I hope Gavin doesn't have someone like that in his life. A surge of protectiveness goes through me, hitting like a damn defenseman on steroids.

"Do you like Charlie?"

He nods, and holds his arm out. "He scratched me once though. It hurt." My entire body stiffens, and his eyes light up, clearly moving on to another subject. "Do you think me and Holden can play hockey with you guys?"

I laugh. "Not sure, bud, but I'll see what I can do, okay?" The door opens up and Harper comes in.

"How about we go for ice cream?" she says.

"Mommy, I'm going to play hockey with Liam."

She smiles at her son. "I think you might have to learn to skate first."

Gavin jumps up, and I push to my feet. "Mommy, can I get skates?"

"I'm not sure." She avoids my glance, and I get the sense that skates just might not be in their budget. "We'll see, okay?"

"You know what, Gavin? My mother kept all my skates, and I bet I can find a pair that fit you."

His eyes nearly bug out of his head. "Really?"

"Really," I say, and he starts jumping up and down. "If it's okay with your mom."

Harper gives me a soft smile full of gratitude and my chest tightens in response. I don't know much about Harper, or anything really, but everything in my gut tells me she's been carrying the world on her shoulders for a very long time. Damned if I don't want to take the load off for her.

"That's very kind. I appreciate it. We'll buy them from you."

"Nah," I say making light of it. "I think Mom was keeping them for when I had a son of my own, and since that's not ever going to happen, they should go to my little brother. Right, Gavin?"

"Right," he says, and when he puts his tiny hand in mine, I swear to God, the universe just flipped me on my head. My pulse beats a little faster in my throat, the degree of responsibility I have here closing in on me.

You've got this, dude.

Worry dances in Harper's eyes as she looks at our joined hands, and in that moment, I swear to God that I'm going to do the right thing here. "You don't want kids of your own?" she asks.

I shrug it off. Since I don't know her, I'm not about to tell her that women don't want the real me. They want the guy I pretend to be, and man, that act is hard to pull off twenty-four-seven. If they knew I was basically an introvert living in an extrovert world, and that I prefer quiet nights and books over parting and drinking, they wouldn't want anything to do with me. That quiet little boy from my youth, the boy who was bullied until I beat the crap out of a guy during a high school hockey game and changed the playing field, still lives inside me.

"Did you say something about ice cream?" I ask, taking a cue from my little brother, and changing the subject.

Harper eyes me for a second and lets it go. "You don't have to come if you don't want to. Today was just an orientation, and we can set up a schedule later."

"You think I'm going to miss out on ice cream?" I say.

"Ice cream. Ice cream. Ice cream," Gavin chants and when I join in, Harper rolls her eyes.

"Did I just take on another child?" she asks with a grin.

"Oh, you two are so perfect for each other," Rita says and when I glance at her, she's looking back and forth between

Harper and me. Of course, she must mean me and Gavin, though. Right?

"All right, let's get ice cream," Harper says, and Gavin and I follow her out the door.

We step into the sunshine, and I glance left and then right. "Should we walk?"

"Yeah, let's go to Stanley park, just around the corner. Gavin likes it there."

"Liam, do you have a dog?" Gavin asks.

"No. Do you?"

"I have a hundred dogs," he says, and I raise a brow. I guess that's why Harper's dress is covered in dog hair all the time.

"Are you like one of the crazy old cat ladies but with dogs?" I ask.

"First, I don't appreciate being called old," she says with a laugh. "And second, no. I'm a dog groomer and dog walker."

The pieces of the puzzle click. "Ah, so Mr. Show and Tell Charlie is a dog, not an uncle."

She crinkles her nose. "Not sure what you mean, but yes, Charlie is a dog, one of many I take care of."

"And Miss Tammy?"

"Preschool teacher."

"So, Charlie is your favorite, huh?"

Her soft chuckle curls around me, settling in places I really wish it wouldn't. I can't sleep with this woman, especially now that I'm her kid's big brother. "My son tells too many secrets."

Gavin lets go of my hand and skips ahead. "Now that I'm Gavin's big brother, am I your favorite hockey player?"

"I don't have a favorite. I don't watch hockey, remember?"

I feign exasperation, and throw my hands in the air. "How come I'm never anyone's favorite?"

This makes her laugh, and she says, "I'm surprised you're not the favorite. Everyone likes a bad boy."

"You think I'm a bad boy?" I tease, or maybe what I'm really doing is flirting.

She goes quiet for a second, her steps slowing as her gaze moves over me, studying, assessing, looking deeper into my soul than any woman ever has before. I shift, uncomfortable under her scrutiny. Jesus, what is she thinking? From her dark, contemplative look, maybe I don't want to know. Then again, how bad can it be? She's put her son in my care. Is it possible this woman sees the real me? I'm cleaning up my act, but the truth is, who I'm displaying right now with her and Gavin is the guy I really am. No showboating, no obnoxious behavior, no loudmouth, foul mouth conduct. Does she like that guy?

"Aren't you, Liam? Are you a bad boy? You are kind of known as the Rule Breaker, aren't you?" she says, the question taking me by surprise.

I scrub my chin, my gaze roaming over her pretty face. Honestly, I can't understand how this woman is single. Guys must be lining up to date her. Heck, for all I know she is dating, or taken, or maybe she's been hurt, and when it comes to her personal life, she proceeds with caution. She definitely proceeded with caution with Gavin and me.

"You tell me," I say, wanting to hear her answer as much as I don't.

"I will, but it will have to wait." She points ahead and I turn to see Gavin standing outside the ice cream shop. A group of young girls, maybe in their late teens or early twenties, step around him and head inside.

"Come on, there's a big line." Gavin shouts. We hurry to catch up with him and I open the door and wave them in. I tug my hat low, but the second we enter, a hush goes through the crowd. Phones are instantly pulled from pockets and aimed my way. And what do I do? I instantly go into Rule Breaker character.

But first I toss an apologetic smile Harper's way. "Sorry." That's when I notice she's gone a bit pale. I'm about to ask what's wrong, but she backs up a bit and takes her son's hand. Before I can reach out to her, I'm surrounded by girls, all wanting their picture taken with me. "Harper," I begin, wanting to check in and see if this is okay with her. She's probably having second thoughts about me and Gavin. Worried that I'll lose him in a crowd if I get swarmed. To show her I'm responsible, I put my hands up and back off.

"I'm here with my little brother today," I say and hold my hand out to Gavin. I meet Harper's eyes and she hesitates for a brief second before she lets him go. He comes to me, and I pick him up and put him on my shoulders. He squeals in delight. A lot of oohs and awws come from the girls.

Presenting my bad boy hockey character, I smile for the girls and raise my voice when I say, "I'll be happy to give you an autograph and a pic, then I need to get this guy ice cream." I spend the next few minutes signing my name on napkins and notebooks, and joking and smiling for the pictures. The girls eventually get their ice creams and head out, but I have to say, these kinds of things always leave me exhausted inside.

"Is it always like that?" Harper asks when the frenzy dies down.

"I promise I won't lose sight of Gavin in the shuffle, Harper. You have my word on that."

She nods. "You were gracious to them."

I shrug. "Have to keep the fans happy."

"Does all that attention bother you?" she asks, her nose scrunched, her expressive eyes assessing me, not looking at me but through me, and I gulp. Can this woman see the guy beneath the charade?

"Why do you ask?"

"I don't know. You seem a bit different around your fans."

"Ice cream," Gavin blurts out, still on my shoulders and I pick him up and put him on the floor.

"What's your favorite flavor?" I ask, and from the way Harper is looking at me, it's clear she's aware I didn't really answer.

"I like rainbow," Gavin says.

"Me too."

"Really?" he asks. "Mommy doesn't like it."

I glance at Harper. "Let me guess, chocolate."

"Actually, vanilla," she says, and my thoughts race, go off in another direction they probably shouldn't go. But you know what, vanilla suits her, and I think that's why I'm so intrigued by her. She's different from all the other women in my world. She doesn't have a face full of make-up, isn't really put together, and could care less about impressing me. My God, is it vanilla I've really been after all these years? Maybe I should take a taste and try.

"Vanilla it is," I say.

I order all the cones, and we step back out into the sunshine. I take a lick of mine. "So good," I say. I hold it out to Harper. "Want to try?"

"No, it's disgusting."

I laugh, as she holds hers out to me. "Try mine."

I take a lick and flash her a smile. My gaze drops to her lips as I swipe my tongue over my own. "I never knew vanilla could be so delicious."

She gulps, like she's not sure if I'm talking about her ice cream, or what I think she'll be like between the sheets. Either way, I want more.

HARPER

"My God, Charlie, you need to cut down on the treats," I say as I maneuver the big retriever in the shower area, and try to wash the soap off his body, but he refuses to lift his backside, which is totally weighing him down. "You need to go on a diet, boy."

"Mommy, when will Liam be here?" Gavin asks, as he plays with his cars on the floor beside me, his duffle bag at his side. Since Liam is taking him to the rink today, I packed him his hat, mitts, a big sweater, and his bicycle helmet. I take my eyes off Charlie for one second so I can check the time, and sure enough, he gives a big shake and splatters me with soapsuds. Laughter from a young boy—my son—and a grown man —Liam—reach my ears, and a thrill goes through me that he showed up, that he hasn't let my boy down. I turn to find Liam walking down the pet store aisle toward me, his lips turned up at the corners.

"Not funny," I say. I wipe my face with the back of my hand, but only manage to get soap in my eye. I swear to God this man has only ever seen me when I was in a rush, harried, shocked, or full of soap. In other words, he's only ever seen me at my worst. I honestly can't remember the last time I primped for anything. These days involve boys and dogs, and they don't care what I look like. I'm sure Liam doesn't either. I see the girls he goes after. All gorgeous and model thin.

But you saw the lust in his eyes when he looked at you, Harper.

Maybe he wants to go slumming for a change. "God, that stings." I turn the nozzle to my face to wash my eye out and the next thing I know, Liam is right beside me, standing in the shower, getting himself wet as he places a paper towel over my burning eyeball.

"This should help." He holds the compress to my eyelid until it stops hurting, and when I finally open it, I let my gaze fall from his handsome face, and take pleasure in his snug shirt and body-hugging jeans that show thick thigh muscles. Damn, how is it possible that in two days he became hotter?

"You're all wet," I say and gulp, because damn, that came out sounding far too sexual.

"You are too."

Oh, he has no idea.

"I have a spare change of clothes, you don't."

"I do at home. I guess I can make a quick stop."

I sigh, and turn the hose back on Charlie. "If you want to go change, we can reschedule." Gavin will be disappointed, but Liam can't take him out while soaked.

"Nah, it's just water. It's a nice day and I'll dry. You still want to go to the rink, Gavin?"

"Yes!" he squeals.

"Okay well, you're not going to the rink like that." I point to his wet pants. "Your clothes will freeze on you."

"You're probably right. Gavin, do you mind if we stop at my place for a change of clothes first, and I have a surprise for you."

"I like surprises."

I finish with Charlie, wrap him in a big towel and dry him.

"So, this is Charlie, huh?" He rubs Charlie's head and when he leans in too close, he gets a big tongue across the face. "Nice to meet you too, boy."

I like that he's not angry or disgusted. My ex hated—wait, no I am not going to think about him. It's a lovely Sunday afternoon, and after Liam takes Gavin to the rink, I plan to do... nothing. That almost makes me laugh. I have a whole afternoon to myself, and you'd think I'd be looking forward to that. I mean, I have a million things I could do, mainly clean the house, prep meals, laundry. Seriously though, none of that sounds like a great way to spend a Sunday. Sundays are supposed to be fun days.

"What are you doing after this?" Liam asks. Jeez, did he just read my mind or something?

"I think there is a book with my name on it."

His eyes light. "You like to read?"

"Yeah, why, do you?" I ask, and he frowns. It's an easy question. I'm not sure why it's stumping him.

"I don't get to read as much as I used to. What kind of books do you like?" he asks.

"Charlie, my boy. Look at you," Mr. Lancaster says as he walks to the back of the pet store, his cane banging on the tile. "How's my handsome boy?" He glances at me. "He didn't give you any trouble, did he?"

"He was the perfect gentleman as always," I tell him. His smile lights up his face, and the lines around his eyes crinkle. He lost his wife a couple years back and Charlie is his pride and joy. "I wanted to talk to you about his diet, though."

"My boy's not fat, he's just big boned."

Liam and I both laugh at that, and Mr. Lancaster turns, and his hand goes to his chest when he recognizes Liam.

"My Lord, you're Liam Dalton."

"Nice to meet you," Liam says, and Gavin jumps from one foot to the other, anxious to go.

"Liam is going to play hockey with me."

"You are a lucky young man," Mr. Lancaster says, and I leash up Charlie and hand him over. "You keep up the good work out there, Liam. Bring us the cup this year." With that he saunters off, and Liam smiles at me.

"No pressure, huh?"

I wipe myself with a dry towel, and drop to my knees to talk to Gavin. "You remember. Be good today and listen to Liam."

"I will," he says with an eye roll.

"If you're not busy, why don't you join us."

"I...I haven't been on skates in forever, Liam, and I know nothing about hockey."

"You don't need to know anything about hockey. A bunch of the guys and I rented the rink for the afternoon, and their wives and kids will be there." He leans in and whispers, "Gavin is going to meet Cole. I think you might want to see the look on his face for that one."

"Seriously? He's going to go crazy." My heart tightens. "This is so nice of you, Liam."

"Every now and then I can do nice," he says with a laugh that reminds me of his on and off ice handle.

"I can't. I don't have skates."

He glances at my feet. "No pressure, if you don't want to, but I have ladies' skates in the car. Size seven, eight and nine. Any of those fit you?"

A weird, almost jealous sensation grips me, and I have no idea why. "All your girlfriends' skates?" I ask.

"Sisters. Mom doesn't throw out anything. I have a couple of my old pairs for Gavin to try on, and like I said, no pressure, but if you'd like to come along, we'd love to have you. Isn't that right, Gavin?"

"Come, Mommy."

I throw my hands up. "Okay then. Give me two seconds to change and I'll be right back." I hurry to the staff room, pull a clean pair of jeans and a T-shirt from my locker and quickly hurry into them. A commotion at the front of the store easily lets me know where Liam and Gavin are and that my son's big brother is a superstar. I stand back and let him do his thing and once the crowd clears, and no one is looking, I note the way he takes a big breath and lets it out slowly. Did that just drain him? I'm pretty introverted myself, so I know what giving of myself can cost me, but Liam isn't anything like me. He's a rebel, a rule breaker, a guy who loves all the attention, right?

"All set?" I ask, and a huge smile materializes, giving me the impression that he's really excited that I'm tagging along, and that maybe...just maybe...he doesn't have to try to put on a show in front of me. Truthfully, I'm impressed with the way he is with Gavin, but he clearly doesn't feel the need to impress me, because there isn't, and can never be, an us. I'm totally okay with that. Yeah, last night I did not lay in bed and think about him as I drifted off. Nope, totally did not work through a fantasy or two of him being on top of me, beneath me, inside me.

"Harper?" I blink as he waves his hand in front of me. "You with me?"

I laugh to hide the color that is no doubt crawling into my cheeks. "Sorry, just thinking about some things I need to do tomorrow. Let's get out of here."

I wave to Mary, the store manager, and head out into the sunshine with my favorite guy, and a guy I am really starting to like.

"Want to hop in my truck?" he asks as he hikes Gavin's duffle bag higher on his shoulder. "I can bring you back to yours later."

"Sure."

Between us, Gavin captures both our hands. "Swing me," he says, and my heart does a funny little tumble as we swing him between us, like we're a real couple, a family...like I always see in those chick flicks I watch. This is what Gavin deserves. A mother and a father, but not just any father. He needs a man who is going to stick around and love him unconditionally. I'm not saying Liam is that man or that I want him to be. I just met him, but someday, maybe it will happen. Once I stop being so afraid of putting myself out there.

We step up to Liam's four-door truck and Gavin's eyes go wide. "This is your truck?" he asks, as I take it in, knowing nothing about vehicles. Heck, Gavin knows more about them than I do. As the guys talk trucks, and I find it so incredibly amusing, Liam opens the back door, and that's when I realize I need to run back to my car to get Gavin's booster seat.

"He needs a seat. I'll be right back." I'm about to dart away, when Liam captures my arm, wrapping his big hand around me. Warm and wicked sensations race through me, and I take a little breath. "What?"

"I already have one. Got it from my sister."

My heart misses a little beat. I honestly can't believe he thought of everything. "Do you always come this prepared?"

"I guess so," he says, and his gaze drops to my mouth and for a brief second, I can't help but think of sex. Yeah, this guy is probably always prepared for sex. If I open his glove box, will I find a huge box of condoms?

"You're a great big brother," I tell him. "You'll be a great dad someday too, Liam."

He doesn't respond. Instead, he turns, and lifts Gavin until he's in the back seat. "I bet you don't need any help buckling in, do you?"

"Nope." Gavin grabs the seat belt and snaps himself in.

Liam winks at him. "So smart," he says, and Gavin just beams under his compliment.

Liam opens the passenger door for me. "Do you need a boost up too?"

"I'm not that short." He just snickers, because yeah, I am short. I lift my leg, struggle a bit, and the next thing I know, his big hands span my ribcage, and he helps me in. I settle into the seat, barely able to spare him a glance as the heat from his fingers careens through my blood and settles deep between my legs.

Maybe my friends are right. Maybe I should brush off the 'beaver-can't do' and have a little fun with this guy. Would that affect his relationship with Gavin? Yeah, it probably would, and Gavin always has to come first.

When do you get to come first?

Oh, when I use my vibrator. That thought brings a small smile to my face, and I can't seem to take my eyes off Liam as he circles the front of his big truck and jumps into the driver's seat.

"This thing is huge," I say, and bite my tongue before I comment on my own observations with something like that's what she said.

"It's not so bad," he says and starts the ignition. "What do you drive?"

"Just a small car," I say. One that's been going for years and is held together with duct tape and a prayer. But he doesn't need to know any of that.

He pulls into traffic and heads north. "My place isn't too far from the rink. I'll change fast." I nod, and as he stares straight ahead, I take in his profile, and the scars on his face. It's not fair for a guy to be that good looking. No, what's not fair is a guy that good looking and I can never hook up. Right?

I sit back in comfort, as he adjusts the mirror. "Hey Gavin, there's going to be some kids at the rink too, and maybe next time we can bring Holden."

I don't need to turn to know his eyes are wide. "That will be fun. Holden is my best friend."

"I know." He turns to me and winks, keeping the secret that Cole will be there. A few minutes later, we pull off the main road and head toward the expensive area of town. We pass by mansions and he pulls up to his house.

"Wow," Gavin says from the back seat, mimicking what I feel inside.

"You live here?"

"Yeah, you want to come in for a minute?"

I reach for my buckle, wanting to get a glimpse into this man's life. "It's huge," I say again, and bite the inside of my cheek, because suddenly no matter what I say, it sounds sexual in my stupid lust-induced brain. But that's because I had to endure sitting next to a man oozing pheromones the whole drive here.

"Yeah, it's big for one person."

He goes quiet, a hint of sadness in his eyes as he pulls his key from his pocket. Gavin jumps down from the back seat. We follow Liam up to the door and he opens it and gestures for us to enter.

Gavin runs in. "This is bigger than my school."

Liam ruffles Gavin's hair. "Go ahead and look around if you like. I'm just going to get changed."

He takes off upstairs, and I stand there, not knowing where to start. "Mommy, look. He has a huge TV."

I follow Gavin into the living room and glance around. The place is actually cozy, pictures on the wall, and throw blankets on the sofa. It seems to have a woman's touch to it. Was it professionally decorated, or did he have one of his many girl-friends help him pull it together for him? Not that it's any of my business. I don't really care. One thing I do care about though, is the bookshelf, and all the colorful spines. He really is a reader, and I'm honestly shocked by that. As Gavin marvels at the too big TV, something that reminds me we really are from different worlds, I take a peek at the books and pull out a crime novel. I grin, loving that this guy is a reader. Or maybe the books are just for show, to impress the ladies.

"See something you like?" Liam asks from behind.

I spin, and as soon as I see him standing there in his low-slung jeans and dry T-shirt that accentuates broad shoulders and a hard body, one thought hits. I want to sleep with my son's big brother, which sounds wrong, dirty and completely inappropriate.

I open my mouth about to tell him just that, when one working brain cell pings me.

Don't do it, Harper. Close your mouth. Walk away. Don't give the wrong idea, or the right idea, or let him think what's about to come out of your mouth next has nothing to do about the book in your hand and everything about the guy standing before you.

I take a deep breath and let my gaze rake over his body as I slowly release it. "Yeah, I do."

5

LIAM

My muscles tighten, one in particular as her gaze drinks me in like I'm a great big frozen margarita and she's been in the desert for weeks. Okay, she clearly likes what she sees, and damn, so do I, but hooking up with her is wrong, right? I'm supposed to be cleaning up my image, not sleeping with every gorgeous girl in my orbit.

"Can we go skate now?" Gavin asks.

"You bet," I say, and clear my throat, because wow, was that my voice? Harper turns and slides the book back into its spot. The truth is I don't usually invite single, eligible women into my home, don't show this side of myself to anyone. So why am I doing it with Harper? I guess maybe because we have a different relationship. She doesn't even like hockey. She only knows my reputation by what she's read about me, and I don't have to be the Rule Breaker around her.

"I grabbed you a sweater," I tell her, and hold it out to her. "Gavin, you have one packed in your duffle bag, right?"

"He does," she says as she pulls my big sweater over her head. It's big and floppy and she couldn't possibly look more adorable. I stare a little too long, unable to tear my gaze away until Gavin speaks.

"I don't want to wear a sweater," he pouts.

"You will when we get there." We head back outside, and I drive the short distance to the rink. Gavin makes fire engine noises in the back when we pass the station, and Harper remains relatively quiet, humming to the songs on the radio. I pull into the parking lot, and recognize the vehicles as I ease my truck into a spot. I bite back a grin, knowing Cole and his family are already here. Gavin is going to lose his mind, and I'm super excited about that. I park and say, "Ready to try some skates on, kiddo?"

He nods and is so rushed trying to unbuckle himself, he can't get the belt off as his little fingers fumble. "Slow down, bud. No hurry."

Harper and I exit the vehicle, and Gavin finally gets himself out and I grab the box of skates and open my tailgate. "Up you two go."

Harper jumps up and I help Gavin. They both look adorable sitting there swinging their legs and I rifle through the box and hand over sizes I think will fit. As they try them on, a news van rolls up.

"What's going on?" Harper asks, a measure of panic in her voice.

"I don't know. Someone probably tipped them off that a bunch of the Shooters rented the rink today. Here to get a story or something. It's no big deal." I put on my game face, ready to play it up when I notice the stiffness in Harper's body, the way her cheeks have paled slightly. What the hell? Come to think of it, she didn't like all the pictures at the ice cream shop either. Is she camera shy, or does she have something to hide?

"You okay?" I ask, as a guy jumps from the van with his camera.

"Yeah, I just... I'm not like you, Liam. I don't enjoy this kind of attention." I eye her, but something doesn't sit right in my gut. There's more to it than that. Before I realize what's happening, we're being recorded. I put my hand up, and step up to the reporter. "Leave them out of this." Damned if that doesn't intrigue him all the more. He looks around my shoulder, but I move to block him.

"Who are they?" the guy asks, refusing to let it go.

"Some friends. I'm involved in the Big Brother program," I tell him, leaving out the part that it's step one in my playboy recovery program.

He gives me a knowing grin. "Yeah? Big Sister, too?"

"Not funny. She's his mother. That's it."

"I bet it is," he says, and I consider it for a moment. Getting photographed with sweet Harper, a pet groomer and dog walker, isn't such a bad thing. Too bad she's not onboard with it. I answer a few more questions, and give him permission to get a few shots of the guys on the rink. No harm can come from it, and it's good publicity for the team.

Once the guy walks away, I give Harper and Gavin plastic blade protectors so they can wear their skates inside. I grab my skates, and Gavin's bag, and toss them over my shoulders. Harper's mood has shifted, her shoulders a little heavier.

"You okay?" I ask, and she nods, putting a smile on her face.

"I haven't skated since I was a kid. Mom and Dad put me in figure skating, and I sucked hard. I begged to get out of it."

I laugh. "You were that bad?"

"After one whole year, I still used the boards to stop, and what I mean by that is I crashed into them, and came to a fast stop. It wasn't what I'd call graceful."

Gavin reaches for my hand, as I toss my arm around her playfully, but the second I do, strange sensations move through me. It feels a little odd. A little real. I can't deny that I envy the guys on my team who've made marriage and family work. "Come on, I'll give you some pointers."

"I don't need pointers." She tucks a strand of hair behind her ear, and that little worried, little vulnerable look on her face punches me in the gut. "I need a miracle."

I hug her tighter, drag her closer in an attempt to offer support, but it could also be because I like the feel of her next to me. "I bet there are a lot of things you can do that I can't."

She arches a brow. "Look at you. A hockey player and a therapist. Gavin is getting more than we've bargained for."

I resist the urge to ask if I can give her more than she's bargained for.

"I'm just saying, we're all good at something. You're good with animals. I'd probably forget to feed it or something."

She arches a brow. "Is that something you want to say to the mother of the child you're mentoring?"

"Uh," I cringe. "What I meant..." I scratch my head, trying to get my foot out of my mouth when she laughs and playfully whacks my stomach.

"It's fine, and I'll have you know that if I didn't become a pet groomer, I'd have become a baker. I make a mean lava cake."

"Mommy, can we have a lava cake?" Gavin asks, not missing a thing.

"Well, I have to make one for Jason's upcoming birthday. I can probably sneak you and Holden a piece."

The strangest surge of jealousy goes through me. "Jason?" I ask, sounding like a total, possessive dick, I'm sure.

"Holden's dad. His birthday party is coming up. You should come."

As soon as she says the words, her eyes go wide, like she instantly regrets them. "I mean, I'm sure you're too busy, and that it would be pretty boring for you, and—"

"Sure, I'll come. I mean, I can't miss out on this lava cake you're so clearly good at making."

My arm slides from her shoulder, and I miss her closeness as I open the doors to the rink. Cold air rushes over us, and laughter reaches our ears.

"It's just that Jason is a huge fan," she says. "That's why I asked."

I nod, not at all insulted that she wasn't asking because *she* wanted me there. "Am I Jason's favorite?"

"I think so."

"Finally," I say with a laugh.

The corners of her mouth quirk with a grin. "Although, I can't be completely sure."

"Jason likes Jonah best," Gavin kindly clarifies.

I shake my head and laugh at the kid's honesty, which I really like, actually. These two are definitely not going to stroke my ego, that's for sure. "No filters on that one, is there?" I tease. I lead them to the bleachers, so I can tug on my skates. I hand Gavin his bag. "Grab your sweater, bud." It's chilly in the rink so he doesn't protest. Gavin reaches into his bag, and puts on his sweater and helmet.

"You don't happen to have a helmet for me too, do you?" Harper asks, her lashes blinking over worried eyes.

"I can run back out to the truck and get mine if you think you need it. It might be a bit big."

"I'm sure it's huge." I eye her, take in the smile that she's trying to hide, when she adds, "You know, to house that big ego of yours."

My jaw drops playfully. "Who told you that?"

She grins. "I think I'll be okay. I don't plan to venture too far from the boards."

I chuckle as I lace up and stand. "Your folks obviously picked the wrong sport for you." She glances off into the distance when I mention her folks, like she's remembering a happy time.

"My mother figure skated and thought I would be a natural."

"Does she still skate?"

She gives a fast shake of her head. "No, she's gone."

I take her hand in mine. "I'm sorry, Harper. I didn't mean to bring up hurtful memories."

"It's okay, it was long ago. They were in a bad accident, and well..." She gazes at Gavin. "He was only one. It's really a shame they never got to know him, and he never got to know them. They would have loved each other."

I suck in air. That couldn't have been easy for her, losing both her parents at once. "Do you have siblings?"

"No, just me." She puts a smile on her face, and claps her hands to redirect and I guess the trip down memory lane is a hard one for her. Since today is about fun, I plan to make sure she has a lot of it, and Gavin too.

"Okay, let's do this," she says. Just then Cole comes skating over to us, and when Gavin sees him, his mouth drops open and no sounds come.

"Hey Gavin, want to be on my team?"

"You're...you're Cole Cannon," he says and Cole laughs.

"You can just call me Cole."

"Mommy," Gavin says and tugs on Harper's sweater, or rather my sweater that hangs loose on her small frame. "That's Cole Cannon."

"I know. Nice to meet you, Cole," Harper says and holds her hand out.

"Same," he says as we shake hands. His sons Brandon and Casey comes skating up to him. Brandon takes off his helmet and gives Gavin a big smile. My God, it's hard to believe how fast my friend's kids are growing. I still think of Brandon as a three-year-old, but now he's seven and Casey is three and a hell of a skater.

"Girls against boys," Scotty says as he comes over, Daisy right behind him. As the oldest of the crew, she's the tallest and pretty much the bossiest of all the kids.

"We will not be playing boys against girls." She puts one gloved hand on her hip. "Girls can play on boys' teams too, Scotty." Zander, Daisy's father, just shakes his head. That guy is in for a world of hurt when she's a teen.

"That's right, they can," Cole's wife Nina says as she joins the crowd, and after I introduce her to Harper, knowing she and the rest of the women will take Harper under their wing, I say, "Harper, did you know Nina used to be a figure skater?"

"I actually do know," Harper says as Gavin continues to stand there star-struck, his gaze bobbing between Jonah as he skates over, and Zander. The guys and their families have flown to Seattle from Boston a month ago, and spend their summers in their cottages at Wautauga lake. I put my hand on Gavin's helmet as he continues to stare.

"I was in figure skating for a year, but I'm not very good at this, and I remember your name. Now you're a novelist. I have some of your books. A lot of them, actually."

"Oooh, really?" Nina says, and hooks her arm in Harper's, and carefully helps her onto the ice. "Tell me which one is your favorite."

"Be careful with her. I want to return her home in one piece," I call out.

As the women skate off, I stand there and smile. Harper really is wobbly on skates. Quinn comes skating up to the two and takes Harper's other arm. I just love my hockey family. I can always count on these guys and their wives. My stomach tightens, because yeah, they need to be able to count on me too, and I need to start by cleaning up my image.

I help Gavin onto the ice and spend a lot of time getting him used to the skates, but unlike his mother, he's kind of a natural at it. Brandon, Casey, Daisy and Scotty all skate with us, and the girls do a few twirling tricks. Soon enough Rider and his wife Jules and their son Chase show up. Jules isn't on the ice, considering she's almost nine months pregnant.

"This is fun," he says, his smile wide as he glances up at me, and my heart tightens. It's nice that I can make Gavin this happy. I catch Harper's smile as the guys and kids and I all pair up for a fun pick-up game. I don't need to teach Gavin the rules, he already knows them. I'm impressed by that.

We spend the next hour playing and just having fun, and every time I check in on Harper, half the time I find her watching Gavin, the other half her eyes are on me, but every single time, she has a smile on her face. I love seeing her happy like this, and well, I'm man enough to admit I like her eyes on me, too. After a while, the women head off the ice, and Jules and Quinn take off while Nina and Harper stay back. No doubt talking about books and Nina had better not tell Harper that I've read some of her romances. All the guys have. It's our little secret.

As our time at the rink dies down, I skate back over to the girls, Gavin's hand in mine, and in walks Jules and Quinn with coffee, donuts and juice boxes for all. My gaze falls to Harper, who is still smiling. I like that she likes my friends, that she's comfortable with them all.

As we dig into the sweets, Harper wobbles around on her skates, and I dart out to the car and grab their shoes. She gives me a grateful smile and changes footwear, and I help Gavin unlace his skates.

"What do you think, Harper?" Nina says. "Want to come?"

"Come where?" I ask.

"Not your business, Liam," Jules says, waving a dismissive finger my way.

"I remember when I used to like you," I tease, and she whacks me as Rider grabs me and puts me into a headlock.

"That's my wife you're talking to." The kids all laugh as Rider rubs his knuckles over my head, and I just play along, enjoying the comradery.

"Well, whatever it is you're planning had better not involve me," I say as Rider lets me go. I sort of overheard something about a surprise birthday party, and to be honest, I'd just prefer a quiet night alone.

"Oh, please, Liam. The world does not revolve around you," Nina says.

I just shake my head and finish my coffee. Once we're done, I scoop up the three pairs of skates. "Ready to go?" I ask.

Gavin stifles a yawn. "Someone is going to sleep well tonight," I say.

"Yeah, me," Harper says and puts her hand over her mouth as she yawns. "We were up early today."

As everyone heads out, we begin to follow, but then Harper stops. "Gavin's bag," she says, and turns. She heads back to the bleachers and when she goes to pick it up, she slips on something, her feet going out beneath her, and the next thing I know, she's flat out on the floor, groaning in agony.

Oh fuck.

HARPER

Flat out on my back, on the cold rink floor, I bring my leg up, and groan as I wrap my fingers around my ankle. The next thing I know, Liam is right there, kneeling over me, and in that moment, I shut my eyes and pray the ground will open up and swallow me. How freaking embarrassing. I just hope no one else was around to see it.

"Harper, are you okay?" Nina says, as she comes running back, and I put my hand over my face, not wanting anyone to see me like this. As everyone comes rushing back, Gavin takes my hands from my face. He cups my cheeks with his little palms.

"Mommy, are you hurt?"

"Just my pride," I say, and he crinkles his nose. "I'm okay. I slipped."

"One of the kids must have spilled their juice," Nina says as she grabs tissues from her purse and wipes up the liquid. "I'm so sorry."

"Not your fault. It's no one's fault. Just an accident." I put pressure on my ankle and wince.

"I think we need to get you to emergency." Liam's eyes narrow. "You might have broken your ankle."

I give a fast shake of my head, and the room spins a bit. Damn, do I have a concussion? "I'm sure it's just sprained."

"Can I have a look?" Jules asks, and I remember her telling me she was a nurse.

"I think it's okay."

She drops down, and checks my eyes. "Does your head hurt?"

"No, I didn't hit it hard." With her brows raised, she checks my head, then turns her attention to my foot. "Does it hurt here?" she asks and applies a bit of pressure.

"Yeah a bit." She does a thorough examination, and sets my foot on her lap.

"I think it's just sprained." She looks into my eyes again, checking my pupils a second time. "I'd suggest staying off it for a couple of days."

"I can't," I say quickly, too quickly judging by the curious stares. "I mean, Gavin, he's busy." It's true, he is, but I can't miss time from work. I have bills to pay, a business to save for.

"Don't worry about Gavin." I turn to Liam as he speaks. "I can take care of him."

"I can't ask you to do that," I say quickly.

"You didn't, and hey, isn't that what big brothers are for."

"Big brothers are for giving wedgies and embarrassing you," Rider says. "Big sisters too."

As everyone chuckles, Liam holds his hand out to me. "Do you want to try to walk, or do you want me to carry you to the truck?"

"Walk," I say quickly. Good Lord, I already look the fool. I can't imagine being carried out of here. I put my hand in his and he carefully lifts me. I set my foot on the floor, and apply a bit of pressure. I do my very best not to wince, but Liam clearly isn't buying it.

"Okay, that's it," he says and scoops me up. Nina takes her son's hand as well as Gavin's.

"Gavin can drive back with us. You get Harper into the truck, and we'll meet you at your place, Liam."

I'm so not used to other people making decisions for me, whether they're good or bad, so I say, "I'm sure I'll be okay, and I need to get my car. I left it at work."

"That will be all taken care of," Liam explains as my hands slide around his neck to hold on. He carries me outside, and I note the news van is still there. The guy was creeping around inside earlier, but I'm pretty sure he didn't get any pictures of me with Liam. That's all I need. If pictures of Liam and me were printed, it would only result in trouble for me.

Liam sets me in the car, and buckles me in. I angle my head. "My ankle is hurt, not my arm. I'm quite capable of buckling in."

"And I'm quite capable of buckling you." He grabs the booster seat from the back and hands it to Nina. "Thanks."

"I think he'll enjoy driving with Brandon and Casey. Do you need me to stop for anything?" Nina asks me.

Oh, just my dignity...

Liam circles the car and jumps in. His brow is furrowed.

"What?" I ask.

"I trust Jules's diagnosis, but maybe we should go to the hospital. Get an x-ray."

I honestly don't have money to spare on a checkup, when I'm certain it's not broken. "I think I'd be better off just to go home and put some ice on it."

He thinks about that for a second and then nods. "Okay." He starts the truck and I catch sight of Gavin, smiling and happy to be with Brandon and his little brother. He obviously admires the older boy and to be honest, all the kids were so great with him, so open and inviting. That thought makes my stomach tighten. The last two men in Gavin's life walked out on him. If Liam decides being a big brother isn't for him, and Gavin loses all these new friends, it will gut him.

I shake my head, and work to push off old insecurities. It's not fair that I'm judging Liam like that. He's been nothing but nice to us, and doesn't deserve to be placed in the same box as the last two guys in my life.

"We should probably go straight to my place. I have to get dinner prepared, and get ready for work tomorrow."

Liam casts me a quick glance. "Who takes care of Gavin when you work?"

"We have a girl down the road that watches him, and sometimes he goes to Holden's. Holden's mom is a really good friend of mine. Come this fall, Gavin starts kindergarten, so we'll have to figure out new arrangements." I take a breath. "One thing at a time, though."

"You should give your sitter a call. Let her know she won't be needed for the rest of the week or two."

I eye him, but he averts his gaze. "What are you talking about?"

"You see, I'm responsible for you hurting yourself—"

"No, you weren't. I didn't fall on the ice, and that wouldn't have been your fault anyway. I fell on the floor." I roll my eyes. "I never thought a backpack would take me down before skates." I laugh at that, and Liam reaches across the seat, takes my hand in his and gives it a little squeeze.

All righty then.

I gulp as his heat zings through me, and steal a glance at him, taking in his strong profile as he stares straight ahead, the muscles in his jaw clenching like he's chewing on my words.

"Everything okay?"

He looks at me. "No, you're hurt."

My heart squeezes a little, liking how much he cares about my well-being. "It's just a sprain. I'm sure I'll be able to walk on it before the night is over."

"I say you give it until tomorrow."

"I have a son to take care of, Liam. I can't just lay around at home."

"You won't be. You'll be laying around at my place, and I'm going to take care of Gavin." I open my mouth to protest, and his lips quirk as he blasts the radio to drown out my voice.

"Real mature," I yell, but secretly, I like this nurturing side of him. I was right. One day he'll make a good dad. What frightens him about that, though? Why doesn't he want kids of his own someday?

I turn the music down. "Tell me about your sisters?" I ask, wanting to know more about his life, even though I should be keeping a measure of distance.

He taps the steering wheel, and I try not to look at his big hands, try not to think about how they'd feel on my body. "They're all older, and very annoying."

"Do they have kids?"

"Yes, Tanya is the oldest sister, and has a girl, Robyne, and Krista is the middle sister and has a boy, Josh. He's around Gavin's age, I think."

"You think? You don't know how old your nephew is?"

"Yeah, I'm pretty sure he's going on five." He shoots me an adorable grin. "Then there's Bethany. We were the closest growing up. She has a newborn son. I think his name is Jax."

"You think!"

He laughs. "Just messing with you. So, she has Jax, and a daughter, Melody."

Hearing about his siblings warms me inside, and I sink into my seat wanting to hear more. "They're all close."

"We're all pretty close. I just haven't been around much lately. I grabbed the skates earlier, but Mom wasn't happy that I tore out of there."

My stomach squeezes. "Am I keeping you from—"

"No." He casts me a quick glance and smiles, like he's trying to soften the harshness of that one word.

"What about your folks?"

"Mom is a nurse, and so are Tanya and Krista, and Dad is an engineer. Bethany stays at home with her kids."

"Where did you get such mad hockey skills?"

That makes him laugh. "Are you secretly watching my games?"

"No, I just heard Gavin say something like that the other day to Holden."

He snaps his fingers like he's down on his luck. "Dammit, here I was hoping I was secretly your favorite."

"Sounds like you grew up in a great family. Did you have any pets?"

"We had a dog named Hank, and a guinea pig named Butterscotch."

I laugh. "I'm not sure I can remember all the names. Then again, it's not like I'll ever meet your family."

He casually rolls one shoulder. "You might, you never know. They'd probably love to meet you and Gavin." He chuckles. "They don't normally like my choice in women."

"Bunnies?" I ask and can't help but wonder if he brought any to a Sunday barbecue at his folks' place.

"Yeah."

I shift, a bit uncomfortable, and not because of my sore ankle. "If I'm keeping you from—"

"You're not," he says quickly, and turns the music up again, putting an end to my protest. He sings along to the music, badly, and I can't help but shake my head and laugh at him. I glance over my shoulder to see Nina and Cole following in their SUV. Soon enough we pull into Liam's big driveway, and I reach for my door.

"No, you don't," he says and touches my arm again. My God, I wish my body would get itself under control. He's Gavin's big brother, not my big daddy. As soon as that thought enters my head, a laugh bubbles out of me, and Liam goes still.

"What?" I ask.

"You didn't bump your head, did you?"

"No, I'm fine. I was just thinking about something my friend Emma said."

"Care to share?"

"If I do, will you let me go home?" I ask, even though I kind of secretly don't want to.

"No."

I fold my arms like a petulant child. "You know, this could be construed as kidnapping."

His brow lifts. "Your point?"

"You're kind of annoying."

"I'm the youngest of four, remember. I perfected annoying before the age of two, and if you want to argue, we can argue. I'm good at that too."

I close my eyes and shake my head, and his laughter follows him out of the truck. A second later, he's at my door, scooping me into his big, strong arms. Big, strong arms? My

God, did that thought really just go through my brain? Not even Nina would use such a corny line in her book. Seriously though, how is it possible that this guy can reduce my maturity to a fifteen-year-old girl, lusting after the hottest jock in school?

He holds me in his arms, as Cole pulls up beside us. I squirm a little, really wanting him to let me down, when a groan catches in his throat. Not just any groan. Okay, so yeah, it's true, I've been walking around with a 'beaver-can't do' for a very long time now, but I still remember what sound a man makes when he's in agony—sexual agony, that is.

"Can you not squirm like that, please?"

"I think you should put me down."

"Can't."

"Sure you can."

"Can't. There are children in the vicinity, and ah, holding you like this." He briefly closes his eyes. "Look, I'm just going to be honest here. Having your body next to mine like this. It's turning me on, okay? I know you're my little brother's mother...wait, that's not coming out right. Let me try again. You're Gavin's mother, but you're gorgeous, and I'm a guy with a big fucking boner. I should probably apologize, but I'm not going to."

As my body burns with want, I swallow, really loving his honesty. "Any woman's body against you arouses you?" I ask, my voice deep, hoarse...needy.

"No, but yours sure as hell does."

Heat moves into my cheeks and my skin warms all over, and I'm so glad I have on his big sweater, otherwise he'd see the arousal in my nipples. Nina comes over to us, and Cole grabs Gavin's bag. She takes one look at me, and I swear to God she knows. She knows I'm totally into Liam, and he's clearly into me.

"Cole and I were talking in the car," she says.

"What were we—" Cole begins, coming up beside her, as Gavin sits in the car talking to Brandon.

She whacks his stomach, and cuts him off. "I realize you don't know us very well, but we were thinking if you're hurt, it might be good to rest, and just have Liam take care of you. We'd love to have Gavin overnight. I know my boys would love it."

"What do you think, Harper?" Liam asks. "I'd be able to give you my full, undivided attention.

Between my legs?

Oh, God, why did that stupid—delicious—thought pop into my brain?

I strive to keep myself together, and my voice comes out normal and easy when I say, "I don't want to put anyone out."

"Oh, believe me, you wouldn't be putting us out, and if you're worried about Liam, he likes to put out." Her lips quirk at the corner, and Cole, finally cluing into what's going on, scrubs his face to hide his laugh.

Gavin jumps from the car. "Mommy, can I? Can I have a sleepover?"

"You don't have clothes, or a toothbrush or anything."

Nina waves my worries away. "He can borrow Brandon's clothes, and we have spare everything."

Gavin tugs on my sweater. "Mommy, please."

I take a fast breath. "Are you sure, Nina?"

"Positive," she says.

"Liam can swing by to get him tomorrow, whenever. No hurry. You just keep yourself off the foot. Best for you to be on your back." This time she really can't keep her grin away, so she turns the other way and walks over like she's saying something to her kids. I'm glad everyone is getting a kick out of this, all the sexual innuendos, and hey, maybe she's getting ideas for a book, but truthfully, she is rather funny.

"Gavin, you be a good boy."

"Yay!" he squeals, and dashes back to the car.

"Jeez, don't I even get a kiss." He blows me a kiss, and hops back into the car. "Thank you," I say to Cole and Nina.

"Come on, let's get you on your back," Liam says, and then he shakes his head, like he too is sexually flustered by all this talk. "I mean—"

"I know what you mean. Thanks again," I say as Liam carries me to the door, holds me awkwardly as he puts his key in and takes me inside.

"Bed?" he asks.

I resist the urge to scream *yes!* from the top of my lungs. He might only be asking where to deposit me, but I have a feeling we're both thinking about something else, and sleeping with him is a really bad idea.

"I have lots of spare rooms. This house is far too big for just me."

"How about the sofa?" I say, and guess he bought the place as an investment. My little bungalow would fit in his living room. He carries me into the room, energy sizzling between us, stealing the breath from my lungs, and the common sense from my brain.

He sets me down, and hands me the remote. "I'll get some ice."

I stare at his lovely backside, the way his jeans hug him nicely as he disappears around the corner. *Girlfriend, do not think about the fun things you could do with that ice.* Dammit, I'm thinking about it, and liking it far too much.

He comes back, sits on the end of the sofa and carefully puts my leg on his lap. "Can I roll your jeans up?"

I nod, only because I'm pretty certain my voice is going to fail me.

With big, deft hands, he rolls my pantleg up, and while most times I'm running around like a chicken with its head cut off and hardly have any time for self-care, I'm so glad I shaved my legs this morning.

"I'm not hurting you, am I?"

Oh, I bet he could hurt you so good.

"No," I say around a tightening throat as I push Emma out of my brain. Once he gets my pants up, he rolls my sock off, exposing my badly painted toes.

"It doesn't look too swollen," he says, and once again, in his presence, I find myself wanting to shoot back with: that's what she said.

Good God, girl get yourself together.

"That's a good thing."

"Yeah," he says, like he's thinking about other things that swell.

"I need it better by tomorrow. I don't have to work at the pet store, but I do have to walk a few dogs in the afternoon."

"Let's not rush things." He very gently sets the tea towel full of ice on my ankle, and I suck in a small breath as the coolness seeps into my skin. "If you can't walk the dogs tomorrow, I can do it for you."

"It's not as easy as it sounds." Okay, I don't mean to sound like I'm on the defense, but really, I might not have a big corporate career or anything, a job like that wouldn't allow me to spend as much time with Gavin as I do, and I have to be mother and father. Some people look down on me for my choice and for some reason, I really don't want Liam to be one of those guys.

His eyes lift, meet mine, and I swear to God, they've darkened a shade. "I never thought for a second it sounded easy, Harper."

Guilt washes through me. There I go, judging him before I really know him. I must say though, I know he's known as the Rule Breaker, but I love the way he is with his friends, and my little family. I think there really is more to this guy than meets the eye. Something solid and dependable deep inside. Still, I know better than to get involved. Dupe me once, your fault. Dupe me twice, mine. I'm not sure what a third time means, or who is to blame, and I'm not going to find out.

"Sorry, I didn't mean to suggest you did. It's just—"

"That some people really suck."

I laugh at that, everything in my body relaxing, because I think he gets it. "Yeah."

"How did you get into pet grooming and dog walking?"

I settle against the pillow. "I've always loved animals. We had a lot of pets growing up. Everything from goldfish, to hamsters, to sheep and llamas."

"Llama, no shit?" I nod. "Did you grow up on a farm or something?"

"Yeah, I did actually. I grew up on a vegetable farm and we had lots of animals."

"Sounds fun."

"It was," I say with a smile, remembering the happier times. "I started doing work with one of the local vets, just helping him out and dog walking, and it blossomed into coming here and continuing it. Someday I want to open my own business. I would have done it already but—" I stiffen and catch myself before telling him about my ex. We don't know each other well enough, and honestly, I'm not about to drag him into my dark history.

He stares at me for a second, and I really hope he doesn't push the issue. "So someday you hope to do that?"

"Yeah, down the road when the time is right. Most of my focus goes into Gavin right now. When he's older, I'll have more time." He frowns and looks down. "What?" I ask.

"It's a lot, huh, raising a boy on your own?" He shifts the ice, and his fingers brush my ankle. My God, how can such an innocent touch arouse me so much? I must be far more desperate for a man in my bed than I realized.

"It's a lot, but we manage."

He goes quiet again, like he's trying to puzzle something out. "You have no family at all, Harper?"

"I have some relatives out east, but I don't ever see them. I wouldn't even know them if I tripped on them in the street."

"That's not right. Everyone needs someone. My sisters make me nuts, but I'd be lost without them."

"I love that so much. I'm okay, though," I say, my voice a little wobbly as his fingers deliberately trace circles over my calves.

"I know you are, but you're always taking care of others, whether it be Gavin, or all those animals at the store. I guess my question is, who's taking care of you?"

I wet my lips and his gaze drops. Despite the ice on my leg, my body grows hot as need flashes in his eyes.

"I...I take care of me."

"I was thinking, maybe for tonight, I could take care of you." The softness in his voice, the gentleness hidden right there, just below the lust, does the weirdest things to my insides. I realize this guy is a rule breaker, a rebel, but right now in this moment, I'm not sure I care about any of that. If we were talking long term sure, but what is going on between us is lust, pure and simple attraction.

"You are taking care of me," I say even though I'm sure he's talking about something else entirely, and I should just nod and let him get on with taking care of me in ways I'm sure I've never been taken care of before.

"I'm taking care of your ankle, but I was thinking I could take care of the rest of you too."

Okay, I'm not going to play games and have him spell it out for me. I know what he wants, and dammit, I want it too. To hell with the consequences. "I...I think I'd like that."

He leans toward me, brushes his hand over my face, the back of his fingers warm against my skin, and a quiver goes through me, settling deep between my legs. "Is this a good idea, Liam?" I ask as one stupid brain cell rings in warning, refusing to let me abandon common sense—regardless of the fact that I want this, agreed to this—and live in pure bliss here.

"No," he says frankly, and it makes me chuckle.

"Look at you. As honest as Gavin." He arches a brow and I add, "It's not a bad thing, Liam. I really could use some honesty in my life."

He considers that for a moment, and then gives a slow nod. "How about this? How about we have tonight." His gaze moves over my face, no doubt finding concern and lust mixing. "Tomorrow, I go back to being nothing other than Gavin's big brother, but tonight—"

"Tonight, you'll be my big daddy."

A smile spreads across his handsome face. "Big daddy?"

Omg did I really just say that. I put my hand on my cheek, which is warm from lust. "My girlfriend, Emma. The one I mentioned earlier, she suggested you be my big daddy. It's silly."

"Maybe, but something tells me you've been giving it thought."

I bite my lip and squeak out, "Yup."

"My God, I like you," he says with a laugh.

"I like you too."

"What's not to like," he teases, living up to his big ego. His smile falls, and he lightly runs his fingers down my arm.

"I have to make one thing perfectly clear. I'm not looking for anything more. I can't. Been down a bad road and won't go down it again, Liam. It's not that I think you're looking for more, but—"

"Can I take you to my bed, Harper?" he asks, his words letting me know we're on the same page here. Relief moves through me to know we only want one thing from each other. At least, I think the rush of blood in my veins is relief. Jeez, it has to be. I'm not going to open myself, or Gavin, up to any more hurt.

"Yes, please," I say, my voice a low, hushed whisper.

He picks me up, and I almost pinch myself. Is this really happening? Lifting me like I weigh no more than his hockey stick, he carries me up the stairs, and into a gigantic master suite. My eyes go straight to his big bed, and I hate that I'm suddenly wondering how many others he's had in that bed before me. I push that thought away. Tonight isn't about anything other than feeling good, and I'm damn well ready for that.

LIAM

My heart crashes against my tight chest as I carry her upstairs, and it's strange that I feel like a teen about to lose his damn virginity. I've been with numerous women over the years, most times after partying and consuming copious amounts of alcohol. After all, I wanted to present the Rule Breaker, the guy the girl of the night wanted between the sheets. Most times, the only way I can draw out that obnoxious guy is to have a drink or four. It usually takes me a full day to recover and gather my energy through alone time. It's not easy being an introvert living in an extroverted world where fans have certain expectations. Maybe the reason why I never brought a woman to my home, to my own bed, was because I needed her gone by morning, so I could recuperate in quiet.

This time, however, I don't know, but it's different. I like this sweet girl who doesn't watch hockey, doesn't expect my on-ice or on-camera antics. She likes the guy beneath the jersey—at least physically.

We enter my room, and she gives a little yelp when I kick the door closed behind me. My cock throbs against my zipper, and while I'd like to ravish her, I won't. She's a goddamn treasure who should be treated with respect and care and I want to take my time with her, give her what she needs, and if I'm being truly honest, I'm excited to be with a girl like her, one who isn't just out to put a notch on her headboard. Yeah, guys don't just do that, puck bunnies do too, and she's anything but a girl wanting to sleep with a professional hockey player for the bragging rights.

Another thought hits. Is it possible that I'm after the chase, wanting a girl who isn't throwing herself at me, a girl who isn't using me for her own personal advancement, or am I intrigued because what we're doing here is taboo, considering I'm her son's big brother? Was there something in the fine print about conflict of interest? Jesus, I can't remember, but I know one thing. Wanting her has nothing to do with any of that, and my pull to her is completely unexplainable, so I'm not even going to try. No, I'm just going to give her, and myself, a night to remember.

I set her on the bed, making sure to keep her weight off her sore foot, and stand back to drink her in. My gaze roams her flushed face, and I love that she's not sitting there all coy, her tits out, in a dress barely covering her ass. I really like this girl, and that should scare me more than it does.

I drop down to my knees and shimmy closer, and her little breath falls over my face as she exhales quickly. I can practically hear the pounding of her heart beneath the layers of clothes.

"I need to see you," I say, never so needy in my damn life.

She nods, and I grip the hem of my shirt, still on her body. She lifts her hands for me, and I peel it over her head, to expose her cleavage, which is rising and falling rapidly as she takes fast shallow breaths. I love that she wants this as much as I do. She wets her lips and I groan. My God, how many times have I thought about taking her mouth with mine, devouring her until she's delirious with want and I can no longer see straight?

Wait, is it possible that I have this too built up in my head, that she can't possibly live up to the fantasy that's been on repeat in my brain, or will this girl rock my world like no other? I'm leaning toward the latter.

"Liam," she says quietly, almost a whisper, as her hand touches my face, cups it gently. I lean into her warmth, her gentle touch tugging at something deep inside me. Something fierce, and foreign.

I push the word "Yeah," past my tight throat.

"I want...I..."

Clearly she's not a woman who has an easy time asking for what she wants, but tonight, that all changes. "Whatever you want, Harper, I'll give you. Don't ever feel shy, or embarrassed to ask. Not with me." If we only have this night, I want honesty with her. Nothing less. "I want to make this good for you." She frowns, and I touch her chin, lift it until her eyes are on mine. "What?"

"I know you've been with a lot of women, and I don't really act or look—"

"Let me stop you right there. You're right. I've been with a lot of women, and none of them were like you, Harper. None of them. If you're worried I'm not going to like this, or you're not going to make it good for me, or live up to those other women, you are dead wrong. The biggest thing you have to worry about is me liking it too much, and wanting more again tomorrow." The worry in her eyes fade, making room for lust and want. "That's better," I say, and I'm about to ask her what she wants, when she speaks.

"Kiss me, please."

She doesn't have to ask me twice. I put my hands on her face, and ever so slowly lean into her until our lips touch and I swear to fuck, her little sigh, combined with the sweetness of her mouth, the softness of her lips, takes me to the ground like I'd just been body-checked. I almost stop, needing a moment of reprieve, to regroup, realign myself and shake off the shockwaves, but I can't bring myself to tear my mouth away.

"Liam," she murmurs, her tongue tentatively sliding inside my mouth. A groan rises from the depths of my throat. I love the sound of my name on her lips when she's aroused, her body pressing against mine, seeking more, everything. I know the feeling of wanting so much it hurts. At least I do now. Before tonight, not so much...

My body tightens, needing this woman in ways that mystify me. My hands fall from her face, and slide down her arms, and if I don't have her completely naked in the next minute, I'm sure my brain is going to explode. I grip the hem of her T-shirt and peel it off and I damn near sob when she sits before me in a white lace bra. I have never seen a woman make innocent white lace sexier. I cup her breasts and lightly brush my thumbs over her nipples.

Her reaction, the little whimper, the way she arches into me, placing her breasts in my hands, mine to do with as I please, sends heat charging through me. The room goes a little dark for a second, the walls closing in on me as blood charges straight to my groin. I take a breath. Jesus, I can't believe I'm about to become unhinged. But if I rush this just because my goddamn dick can't wait to slide inside her and stay there for the rest of the night, I'd have to take myself outside and kick my own ass somehow.

I slide my hands around her ribcage and unhook her bra, and my throat makes a sound as I go back on my heels and take my fill of her gorgeous, plump breasts, her pale pink nipples tight with arousal. I stay like that so long, unmoving, she shifts and is about to cover herself when I take her hands.

"No, I like looking." She nods, and opens her mouth, only to close it again. "We only have tonight, Harper. We might as well take what we need, and ask for what we want."

"I...I like looking too," she says taking me by surprise and I can't help but grin.

"I like that. I like you telling me that." I stand, take a step back and reach over my back to tug off my shirt. Her gaze leaves mine, and I almost peacock around the room at the appreciation in her eyes. I love the way she's admiring me. "More?" I ask.

"Yes, please."

I release the button on my pants, and she sits up a little straighter. She's clearly been with other men—heck, she has a son—but there is so much innocence about her, a vulnerability of sorts, that makes me want to wrap her up in my arms, and protect her...but from what, I don't know. The world? Men who've hurt her? I'm not even sure she's been hurt. But that must have been what she was trying to say when she said she couldn't go down that road again. Rage goes through me to think someone hurt her and her son, but we'll get to the bottom of that another time. Right now, there is another bottom I need to get to.

Zipper down, I slide my fingers into my jeans and tug them off. She puts her hands on her thighs, leans toward me, and says, "Keep going."

I do as she says, and my pulse thumps at her excitement, the heat in her eyes as I tear off my boxer shorts and stand before her in nothing but a smile, and my cock raging hard with need. She crooks her finger, gestures me closer and as much as I want her hands on me, her mouth around my girth, I shake my head no.

For a split second, her mood changes, and she inches back, like she's afraid I might have suddenly changed my mind. A man would have to be declared clinically insane to walk away from her.

"I want to see you. Get out of your clothes."

"Oh," she says, and I let it go. I don't need to ask what was going through her head. She realizes she's not like the girls I usually sleep with, is worried that I might not find her as appealing, and I did my best to soothe her worries with my words. I guess now I'm going to have to sweep away the rest of her uncertainty with my hands.

She stands on both feet, and opens her jeans. "Your foot," I say. "Don't put pressure on it."

"Liam, the only thing I'm feeling right now is pleasure."

I chuckle at that. "But tomorrow, it could start hurting again."

"I'm hurting." She reaches for my hand and I nearly bite off my tongue as she puts it between her legs. "Right here."

"I'm definitely going to do something about that."

She wiggles her hips, and if I'm not mistaken, sweet little sunshine loves how much I'm hurting. Once she has her pants around her knees, I drop to the floor, slide my hand between her silky thighs and just revel in the texture of her skin. She quakes beneath my touch, and I say, "I'll take it from here." Yeah, tonight is all about me taking care of her.

I make her sit back on the bed, not wanting her to put pressure on her ankle as I finish undressing her. With slow movements, wanting to draw this out and savor each second, I drag her pants down until she's in nothing but her matching lacy white underwear. How the fuck did I get so lucky? I must have done something right in a past life because I don't really think I'm doing all that great with this one. Except for right here, right now. Harper in my bed, allowing me to take care of her, that, my friends, is a great decision. Tomorrow, I swear to God, no regrets. I refuse to stress over the right and wrong of it, and I won't let her.

I pull her back up, and place my mouth near her ear, and a fine quiver moves through her when I say, "Put your arms around me to keep the pressure off your ankle." I align my body with hers and press my cock, which is hard as fucking steel, against her body, and she stands there before me, shivering. Needing to smooth her goosebumps, I trail my hand down her neck, her arms, and bend forward to run my fingers up her outer thighs. My entire body is on fire, the need careening through me making it hard to go slow.

"Harper," I say as she stands there, gifting me with her body and allowing me to admire her.

"Yeah."

"Touch me."

Her hand lifts, and she inches back slightly. She touches my face, her lust-imbued gaze on mine, her breathing heaving and shallow. My shoulders curl and my muscles clench as her hand drops to my chest, and she lifts tentative eyes to mine.

"What the fuck are you doing to me?"

"Just touching," she says, and when she sees my physical reaction to a simple touch, she begins a deeper exploration, clearly liking what she does to me. Her hands trail over my chest, my abs, and she stops for a second to take pleasure in the hills and valleys. "You're so hard," she says.

"You have no idea," I tell her, and her head lifts, a grin on her face. With a new bold look about her, her hand trails lower and I nearly shoot off the second she takes my dick into her hand. She weighs it in her palm and the show of appreciation in her eyes fills me with a ridiculous sense of pride.

"I think I have some idea," she says, a little unstable on her feet, and I'm not sure if it's from her ankle or that she really likes what she sees.

"I think you're right. I think I need to get off my ankle." I'm about to nudge her back to the bed, when she sinks to her knees, clearly having something totally different, something totally wicked and delicious, in mind. Her sweet pink tongue snakes out and slides over my swollen crown, and pre-cum pools on the end. She dips into it, and I growl as I fist her hair, not sure whether I want to tear her mouth from my dick, or push her harder against it. That sexy mewling sound makes me impossibly harder, and when she cups my aching balls, a tortured groan tears out of my throat.

"Harper," I whisper. Women have gone down on me in the past, and I've always liked it, so I'm not so sure why I'm practically singing gospel—and I'm not a holy man—simply because she has her lush pink lips wrapped around me. "That's too good."

My head falls forward and she inches back, her mouth open, my cock resting on her bottom lip. "Want me to stop?" she teases, her words jumbled, barely comprehensible with my cock right there.

"Yes," I say even though it's killing me to stop her.

She goes completely still and my cock falls from her mouth, and the almost humiliated look on her face guts me. "You don't like it. I knew—"

"Harper. Don't. You are fucking amazing. I can't even tell you how hard it is for me to stop you, but you need to understand something. I want to take care of you." I gather all my strength, carefully pull her to her feet and nudge her until she's sitting on the bed. She blinks up at me, her cheeks flushed, so goddamn pretty my heart is ready to explode. "I don't come before you. Simple as that."

"Oh."

"Now, spread your legs. I want to see you."

She swallows, excitement dancing in her eyes. Hands on her thighs, she widens her legs, and her pussy lips open to reveal the prettiest shade of pink I've ever set eyes on. Her dampness glistens in the overhead light, and I know in an instant that after one taste, she's going to be an addiction I can't quit. But we only have tonight, and I'll have to take my fill of her and pray it's enough.

I tear my gaze away from her hot pussy, and meet her eyes. "I've wanted my mouth on you from the second I met you."

Those blue eyes widen, almost surprised, and I shake my head. "You have no idea how beautiful you are, do you?"

"I...don't always feel beautiful," she says honestly. "Most times I'm just trying to figure out how to juggle everything and make it through the day."

My heart squeezes at her vulnerability, and I drop before her, putting my hands over hers. I plan to help her, be there for her in the day, and tonight. "Right now, I don't want you to think. I just want you to feel, want you to let me take care of you."

She doesn't say anything. Instead, she sits there blinking up at me, and I lower my head to press my mouth to the needy spot between her legs. I lick her, and her flavor explodes on my tongue, and her hands rake through my hair. I love the way she tastes, and the ways she greedily touches me.

I lick and suck and pull her swollen clit into my mouth, and the whole time, she is writhing beneath me, needy and eager, like she hasn't been touched in a long time, like I'm breaking some long drought that has been sucking the life out of her. I hate that she's been going without, almost as much as I like that she'd chosen me to break her dry spell with.

I move my face around, eat at her, and slide one finger into her tightness. She vibrates around me and I can hardly believe how close she is to erupting all over my finger and mouth. I glance up at her, and hunger builds inside me as she puts her hands behind her on the bed, and lifts her hips, banging her sex against my face.

"Touch your breasts," I say, and she sits up a bit straighter to take them into her hands. "Fuck, you're something."

Her lids fall shut, and I go back to giving her what she needs, what we both need, because I swear I need to pleasure this woman more than I've ever needed anything in my entire fucking life.

Why the fuck isn't that scaring me?

HARPER

I can barely catch my breath, let alone think or even see straight as the man between my legs puts his finger inside me, stroking deeply, thoroughly, his deft tongue ravaging my swollen clit.

"My God, Liam," I cry out, and every time I say his name, moan, or show him how much I'm enjoying it, it seems to drive him to more, like my pleasure is paramount, and I have to say, I've not been with many men, but this is the first time a guy has really brought his A-game, and wanted to put me first.

A girl could get used to this, but we both agreed to one night and I straight up told him I couldn't do more. Not that he wanted more, but I just needed for us to both be in the same head space. Sex and relationships are two very different things.

He inserts another finger and all thoughts dissipate as plea-sure grows, spreads, and overtakes my entire body. A keening sound catches in my throat and I'm sure I can hear mumbled curses as I completely let go, focusing on nothing but the pleasure peaking and breaking between my legs. More curses reach my ears as I rake my hands through his mess of hair and shamelessly hold him to me, buck against his face even—God, this is so not like me—as I come and come and come some more.

My spasms finally die down, and his head lifts. A small smile touches his mouth, but he's no more in control of himself than I am. He might be pretending he's all cool and collected, but his body is shaking, his breathing shallow, his cock rock hard, raring to go. I like that I can do this to him, although I'm not more special than any other woman he's been with, no matter what he says. He's a red-blooded male in his prime, and a raging hockey player at that. Fucking is their number one hobby. Nevertheless, the last time I orgasmed with such ferociousness was...never.

He falls over my body, his cock pressing hard against my thigh. "I love the taste of you," he says and buries his mouth in the crook of my neck, the wetness on his face dampening my skin. His breath is fiery hot against my flesh, scorching me from the inside out. I slide my hands around his back and take pleasure in his rippling muscles.

His mouth finds mine, and his kiss is hungry, filled with raw need, and I might have just orgasmed, but another round of heat races through me, bringing arousal with it.

"I want you inside me," I tell him.

"There's nowhere else I'd rather be," he answers, his rough and raspy voice raking over my skin and bringing a deeper need to my body.

He moves me, positioning me in his bed, and then reaches into his nightstand to pull out a condom. Nice and easy access that makes me think of how many women he's had here before.

Nope, not going to do it.

Instead of thinking about such foolishness, I look at his taut, perfect backside as he shifts and shuts the nightstand drawer. He rips into the condom packet with his teeth, and while some may think it's coarse and crude, it kind of turns me on all the more. Weirdo much?

But I really just don't care. Liam is so easy to be around, so easy to be myself with. He removes the condom from the packet and groans as he sheathes himself, and I just lay there, shaking with excitement, so ready for this. It's a bit shocking, actually. I really don't know him, and yet I'm entrusting him with my son, and my body.

He strokes himself and I watch on with fascination at how uninhibited he is. Everything about this man tears at the layers protecting me and peels away my inhibitions. I'm never so open in the bedroom, and it's such a shame.

His mouth finds mine as he falls over me, his big body spreading my legs as he eases himself in between my thighs. I widen for him as my heart crashes against my chest. I'm about to tell him to be gentle, that it's been so long, when he smooths my hair from my face, and meets my eyes.

"It's been a while, hasn't it?" he asks, the tender understanding in his voice bringing a lump to my face.

"Yes," I say honestly. "Been too busy with life, and my son."

"I know." He presses his lips to mine, and kisses me softly, slowly, as his crown breaches my opening, spreading me a little at a time. I wrap my legs around him, and he gives a tortured moan. "Trying to go slow here, Harper. That's not helping."

I chuckle, a breathy, needy laugh that curls around us. "Sorry. Not sorry."

He gives me another inch and my moan deepens. "You feel so good, Harper."

My sex muscles clench as he pushes into me, so agonizingly slow that I'm sure I'm about to combust. He stretches me in the most glorious ways. My body gives way to his, our fit so perfect it shocks me. I lift my hips to help him along, letting him know I can take all of him and that I needed every inch five minutes ago.

"Fuck me," he growls, and with one hard thrust fills me completely. Breath leaves my lungs as he pushes against my cervix, and a strange, new kind of pleasure takes hold. "You good?" he asks, slowing to check up on me, and I love his self-lessness. He might be a rule breaker, but that doesn't mean he's not caring. I saw that side of him with Gavin. Come to think of it, I only saw his loud side when he was entertaining a crowd, or the news crew. But I'll have to give that deeper consideration later, when his cock isn't inside me.

I lightly rake my nails over his back and his mouth finds mine again as he inches out of me. I lift my hips, urging him back, but he has other ideas. He puts his hand between our bodies, pinning me down as he applies pressure to my clit.

"Oh," I say, willing to stay still if he's going to do this to me. His fingers glide over my clit as he slides in and out of me, and even though it feels incredible, I swear to God, it's the look on his face, a mixture of sweet torture and bliss that propels me into outer space. I clench around him and he bends to take my nipple between his teeth. He clamps down, and then licks the sting, and as pain and pleasure merge, my body once again lets go. I come around his pistoning cock, and my juices make him slick as he puts both hands under my body to grip my shoulders.

"You've got me right there," he growls, his blunt strokes for him now. I lift and meet his pounding cock, his pelvis smashing against my clit, and if I didn't know any better, I'm sure he's going to make me climax again, but three in one night? Impossible, right? Or not.

"Liam," I say, my brain a mushy mess of need and lust, my synapses no longer firing as nothing but pleasure exists in this realm. He hits my cervix, time after time, and before I even know what's happening, I'm coming again as he rides me, hard, fast, prolonging my orgasm as his approaches. He thickens inside me. "I feel you," I cry out as I clench around him, never before having a full body climax and not really even knowing if they existed. Oh, but they do exist and it took this man to teach me that.

He pushes hard and deep and throws his head back, a deep guttural sound in his throat as he comes with me, coming high inside my body. I shatter around him, my entire body shaking like I'd just come from the rinse cycle, and when it stops, I collapse into a quivering mess of pleasure, a goofy smile on my face. He goes still and falls over me, sealing our moist bodies as he breathes against my neck, hot labored pants that speak of pure satisfaction. I smile, unable to contain the happiness welling up inside me.

Our breathing settles and he lifts himself, his eyes meeting mine, assessing me, asking questions that I'm not sure I know answers to. "Are you okay?"

My God, I'm not sure I'll ever be okay again, and if I could go back in time and shake some sense into the me from an hour ago, I would. Why the hell did I agree to only one night? I guess the me from an hour ago had no idea this would be so fantastic, and dammit, I want more.

"I'm good," I say. "Actually, I'm better than good."

"You might not be so good in a second," he says, and my entire body stiffens, my bliss disappearing in a puff.

"What?" I ask, and try to scramble backward, but he pins me with his impressive weight. What on earth does he mean? Was I not as good as he thought I'd be? Did I not live up to his expectations? Judging by the look on his face, however, I'd say those worries are for nothing.

"I fucked up," he said.

"What did you do?" Oh, God, he didn't lose the condom, did he? I can't get pregnant. Not with his child. He does not have long term about him, and neither of us are looking for that.

"I liked it too much," he says, an adorable grin tugging at the corners of his mouth.

A laugh bubbles up inside me. "You're crazy."

"Hey," he teases. "I've been called worse."

"I'm sure you have, and well, if we're being honest here, I might have liked it too much too."

His grins spreads, heat and fire in his eyes as he looks at me, and I'm almost certain he's ready to go for round two. "Are you saying we can do this again? I think we were premature in saying it was a one-night thing. Although I never like to use the word *premature* after sex."

I laugh as he rolls off me, pulling me to the side, but the smile is gone from his face. My stupid heart flutters when he brushes my hair from my shoulders, his gaze moving down to take in my nakedness. Has any man ever looked at me like that before? How do I even describe it? A mix of lust and curiosity? I'm not sure, but it does something weird to me.

As a flurry of excitement dances in my stomach, I say, "I'm not sure it's a good idea, Liam. I think it's a conflict of interest. You're Gavin's big brother, and while it was fun having you as my big daddy," I say, hoping to lighten his mood as well as my own, "I don't think we can do this again."

"You're right. I know it." He shuffles on the bed. "Hang on, I'll be right back." He throws his legs over the bed, removes the condom and dashes into his ensuite. I fight an internal battle as I wait for him. Can we do this again? My God, I'm trying everything to convince myself we can have sex, but inside I know once he's tired of me, he'll bolt and that means leaving Gavin too. No, it's best we keep an arm's length. At least that's what my brain is telling me, but the second he comes back, and presses a warm cloth between my legs to clean me, all common sense packs a bag and heads south for the summer.

Speaking of summer...maybe we can do this while he's home, before he leaves for training camp—at least, that's what I think it's called. Gavin said something about it. I mean, that might be okay, right? He'd be leaving, but not leaving. I mean, our hook-up would be over, but he could still be Gavin's big brother, and we could forget this ever happened. As long as it doesn't affect Gavin...is there a problem with this?

Once I'm clean, he tugs on his T-shirt and jeans, goes to his dresser to get a clean pair of sweats and an oversized shirt for me. "This will be big, but it will be warm."

I test my ankle as I sit, and tug on the shirt. "I've worn more of your clothes today than my own."

He smiles. "I actually like seeing you in my clothes."

"I bet you say that to all the girls," I tease, but I might as well have punched him in the gut. His smile falls, and he rakes his hand through his hair, the disappointed look on his face gutting me. Jeez, what did I say? "I didn't mean—" I begin, but he cuts me off.

"Hungry?"

I eye him, and deep in my gut—from his actions when he's with me and his reactions to some of the things I've said—I'm beginning to believe more and more that I'm seeing a side of him others aren't privy to—and that Liam has a depth few men do. "Actually yeah, and I'd like to give Nina a call to see how Gavin is doing."

"Sure."

I put my feet on the floor and Liam is right there, standing before me, ready to be my legs if I need him to be. I think he might be overreacting, but I kind of like all the attention. How pathetic is that?

"How's the ankle?" I put pressure on it, and while I'm sure I can hobble back down to the kitchen, I wince a little. "That answers my question."

He scoops me up and I feel like a small child milking the situation just to get attention. "I can probably walk," I admit. "But...I kind of like you carrying me."

He laughs at that, and I'm happy to see his smile again. He carries me to the kitchen and sets me on a stool at his gigantic island.

"Your place is so big."

He gives me a playful wink. "Big, yeah, that's the word I like to use after sex."

I shake my head at him, even though I'm happy this easygoing side of him is back. "Big is definitely the word to describe you," I begin, and he lifts a brow. "Big ego."

He chuckles and grabs a stack of menus and spreads them out in front of me. "What do you feel like having?"

Oh, maybe a Big Mac and a side of Liam.

"Everything sounds good, I'm so hungry." He pours me a glass of water and I take a big drink, realizing how parched I am. "How about Thai?"

"Perfect."

I glance around. "Do you have any idea what I did with my purse?" He disappears into the living room and comes back with it. "Thanks." I fish out my phone and he gives me Nina's number before he puts in our order.

Nina reassures me Gavin is having a blast, and I smile when I hang up. I really like Liam's friends, and I love how they took Gavin under their wing. I just pray that I don't do anything to screw it up, and Liam wants to be his big brother for many years to come. I was worried, but he's proving to be a good influence, despite his reputation.

Thirty minutes later, our food arrives, and Liam sits beside me at the island as we dig in. He's quiet and pensive and keeps casting sideways glances at me. "Something on your mind?" I ask.

He shrugs, and his warm scent falls over me. "It's not my business, but I was wondering if Gavin's father is in his life."

The chicken I'd just swallowed lodges in my throat, and I take a big gulp of water to wash it down. "No, he's not, actually."

He nods. "Sorry to hear that."

"I'm not." I drag my fork through the noodles on my plate. "I don't want Gavin around a man who could up and leave without a backward glance, and was cheating on me with a close friend, who is no longer my friend, obviously."

His eyes go dark, almost murderous. "What a bastard, and yeah, I wouldn't want him around a guy like that either."

"We were young. That's not an excuse and I'm not justifying what he did. I'm just glad I had Mom and Dad the first year. I would have been lost without their help."

He takes a big drink of water, his eyes on me. "You've been on your own for a long time."

"Yeah," I say, my mind going back to the man I trusted after Gavin's father left. I really don't want to talk or think about him, and if he ever knew I was with Liam, or that he was Gavin's big brother, it would bring nothing but trouble. An uneasy shiver moves through me, and Liam shifts closer.

"Everything okay?" he asks.

"Actually, no. I think I fucked up," I say, throwing his words back at him.

He angles his head, his curious gaze moving over my face. "Yeah?"

"None of this was a good idea." He gives a curt nod, and is about to pull away, when I put my hand on his arm to stop him. "But it was the best worst mistake I've made."

"So, we can do it again?" he asks, his childlike eagerness filling me with a lightness I haven't felt in years.

"Yes."

9

LIAM

I've been hanging out with Harper and Gavin for a couple of weeks now, helping her at the pet store, and helping her walk all the dogs, and no, it's not easy for me. Although, Gavin gets a kick out of it when I get all tangled in the leashes and fall on my ass. Maybe I do it just to make him smile. I don't know, but I do know I don't have to walk them or help. Harper's ankle is better. I know it. She knows it. But it's a game we're playing and I can't seem to help myself around her. I want to be there for her, do things for her. Maybe it's a dangerous game, but the more time I spend around them, the more I want to be around them, and when I'm not with them, I'm thinking about them.

They've both been staying at my place, and honestly, it's been so easy having them there. For the first time in a long time, I haven't had to put on a show or act like an asshole for adoring fans who expect the worst from me. I haven't even needed alcohol to help me through the day, or find myself in need of escape.

"Can I have a taste?" I ask as Harper puts the last touches on a cake. I reach out, and she whacks my hand.

"You're as bad as Gavin," she says.

Gavin's head lifts at the sound of his name. "Mommy, I want a taste too."

"Fine." She grabs the beaters and hands one to Gavin and the other to me, and as we lick them, she just shakes her head at us. Tonight, I'm going to hang out with her friends, and I'm excited to meet them, although big social gatherings really aren't my thing, but I'll have Harper at my side, so my anxiety isn't too high.

She checks the time. "We should probably get going. Gavin, do you have your bag packed?"

Gavin jumps up and little feet sound on my stairs as he runs up them. Damned if I don't like the sound they make. I stand, and circle the island, stepping up behind Harper. "Stop," she says, as I nuzzle her neck. "Gavin will be back any second."

"I know," I say. "I just can't help myself." Harper has been sleeping in my bed every night, and sneaking out before Gavin wakes, and I have to say, the second she leaves, I miss her presence, the soft little sounds she makes in her sleep. That thought makes me laugh, because it wasn't too long ago that I wanted nothing more than to sneak out under the cover of darkness so I could wake up alone.

Footsteps pound on the stairs, and I back away. "Did I tell you how gorgeous you look?" I say as I take in her little black dress, which has no dog hair on it. Not that I mind the dog hair. It's what makes her special.

"Only one hundred times." She points the spatula at me. "But you know you don't have to flatter me, Liam. I'm kind of a sure thing."

I laugh. "It's not flattery, it's true. You're gorgeous, and you're mine."

"For a little while longer, anyway," she says reminding me we agreed to have a secret hook-up until I leave for training camp. We also agreed that we wouldn't let what was going on between us affect my relationship with Gavin.

"You all ready, kiddo?" I ask, and try not to give any consideration to the knot in my stomach. This is just a hook-up. Neither of us are looking for anything more, right? Just then, my cell pings and I see that it's Jeremy. Christ, it was just the other day he told me it might not be a bad idea if Harper and I were photographed together. He's not wrong. Pictures of the three of us would serve me well, show my fans that I'm cleaning up my life, and give the endorsement company the clean-cut image they're looking for. I just hope my fans will stick with me. While I like to make them happy and give them what they want, all that no longer seems as important as it once did. No, hanging with Harper, seeing life through her eyes, has shown me what's really important in the big scheme of things.

"I have to grab this," I say to Harper, and step into the other room. "Hey, what's up?" I ask when I answer the call.

"Just checking in again to see how things were going with the big brother program. You've been so quiet lately."

"I thought you wanted me to stay out of the papers."

"I wanted you to stay out of trouble." A dog yips in the background, and I have a hard time envisioning Jeremy with a small yappy dog. "You still going to that party tonight?"

I walk through my living room, grab the remote and shut off the game Gavin had been playing. "Yeah, why?"

"Because it's my job to make sure you keep your endorsements."

"Doing my best."

"Have fun, and I'll talk to you later."

I frown. "What the hell was that all about?" I mumble to myself as I end the call. Harper pokes her head in.

"You talking to yourself in here?"

I quickly shove my phone into my pocket as she steps up to me, a curious look on her face.

"Everything okay?" she asks.

"Ah, yeah, I think."

She smooths her hands over my dress shirt and looks like she's about to say something else, but closes her mouth when Gavin comes running in. "Mommy, why can't Holden and I stay here?"

"Because your babysitter doesn't live around here, which means you're going to sleep in your own bed tonight so she can watch you."

"Why can't I live here?" he asks, and her face falls as she ruffles the Shooters hat on Gavin's head. It has jelly stains on it, but he won't take it off to get washed. He sleeps in the thing.

"Because we have our own home." She taps his nose. "I told you, we're only staying here for a bit, because I hurt my ankle and Liam is helping out. Now get your stuff. The babysitter will be at our place soon, and I'll be saving a big piece of this cake for you and Holden."

"But—"

"Gavin," Harper warns, and when he grumbles, I pipe up, unable to handle the sad look on his face. I'm going to be such a pushover when I'm a dad. That thought makes me laugh, because until these two, I never gave much consideration to it before, assuming that women want the Rule Breaker, not the guy I really am.

"Hey, wait a second." I go to the hall closet to grab another hat for Holden. Gavin's eyes light up.

Gavin wraps his hands around my waist and gives me a big hug. "Thanks Liam. I wish you could be my daddy."

My pulse jumps, and I swallow, not knowing how to answer that. It breaks my fucking heart to think his father left without a backward glance. I drop to one knee, and give him a little nudge on the chin. "I'm your big brother," I say.

"I know, but—"

"Gavin, grab your bag," Harper says, cutting him off and he drags his feet when he goes back to the kitchen. Harper sucks in a little breath. "Sorry about that."

"Yeah," is all I say, my brain taking a moment to consider what it would be like to be Gavin's father. Problem is, I'm not really seeing a downside. Jesus, what the hell is wrong with me?

She gives a big sigh. "Maybe staying here wasn't such a great idea. I mean my ankle—"

"No," I say quickly, maybe too quickly judging by the look on her face. "It's just for a little while longer, before I head to training."

She frowns, and I want to grab her and kiss her until she's smiling again, but I can't, not with Gavin walking back into the room. I brush my knuckles against hers and her body physically reacts, and I like that I can do that to her.

She gives me a wobbly smile. "As long as we're not in your way."

"Not in my way," I say, and wink to lighten things. "I like all the perks." She rolls her eyes. "What, don't you?"

"You know I do," she says quietly, then claps her hands. "Okay let's get this show on the road." She grabs the cake and we all head outside.

The second we hit the driveway, I know something isn't right. I glance up and see the news van, and a reporter coming our way as the cameraman captures footage of us all.

"Liam, can I have a minute of your time?"

Beside me, Harper goes stiff, and I take a moment to consider what Jeremy said about the two of us. Had he set this up? Normally I wouldn't care, would play up to the camera for my fans, but Harper isn't okay with this, and I guess I don't blame her. She's a single mom doing her best to raise her son. She didn't sign on for having her face splashed in the papers with mine.

"Not a good time," I say, and he shoves a microphone in my face. I'm about one second from grabbing it and smashing it, but stop when Harper's hand lands on my back.

"You go ahead, Liam. Your fans will want this and it's good for your career. I'll get Gavin into the car. We'll wait for you."

While I appreciate her thoughtfulness, I don't want to put this guy and his interview before her and Gavin. Then again, I have no doubt Jeremy set this up for the exact purpose of cleaning up my image with this wholesome woman and her son. She backs up, takes Gavin's hand, and they both climb into my truck.

"What do you want to know?"

"Who's the new lady and boy in your life?" he asks, as he holds the microphone inches from my mouth.

I snort. "Friends, and I'm sure you already know who they are." This is the media; they would have done their research.

"What's the cake for? You going to a party?"

"Yes, and I have to go. If you want an interview to talk about hockey, check with the team's publicist."

I don't like the grin on his face as he backs away, and I slide into the driver's seat and note the tightness in Harper's shoulders. I glance in the rearview mirror as the guy climbs back in his van.

"You okay?" I ask and put my hand on her arm.

"I really don't want my face in the paper with yours, Liam," she says, and I try not to react like she just kicked me in the nuts. But I get it. I have a reputation, and she doesn't want to get mixed up with me—outside the bedroom anyway.

"I'm sorry. I wasn't behind that."

"I didn't think you were. I just…I can't be photographed with you." She bites her lip, and stares straight ahead and I get the sense that she wants to say more on the subject, but then she glances at the dashboard clock and says, "We should get going."

My stomach is tight, uneasy as I drive to her friends' place and wait in the car as she runs in to get Holden. On one hand, I can't blame her for not wanting to be seen in public with me, coming from my house in a situation that could be deemed intimate, but on the other hand, it rips a goddamn hole in my gut.

In the back seat, Gavin talks endlessly about the video games they're going to play tonight, and I glance around the cute neighborhood. It's mostly small bungalows, with basketball and hockey nets, and toys left in the driveway for another day's play. I find myself smiling because it reminds me of the way I grew up. I bet Mom and Dad and all my annoying sisters would love Harper and Gavin. Mom's been after me to come home for a Sunday dinner, and I guess I should make a point to do that before August and I'm gone.

I shake off the troubled feeling coursing through me as Holden comes running to the car, and he stops at the driver's side door. I've yet to meet him, and I wonder if he's going to tell me Alek is his favorite. I open my door. "Hey buddy," I say, and he just stands there and smiles at me. I gesture to the back seat. "Hop in, Gavin has something for you."

Harper sets his booster seat into the back and he's talking nonstop as he jumps in and the look on his face when Gavin hands him the hat is priceless.

Harper slides into the passenger seat. "I think he likes it."

"No kidding."

I drive them the short distance to Harper's place and she jumps out with the boys to meet the sitter. A few minutes later, she's back in the car with me, and I lean into her, catching her by surprise, and press my lips to hers.

"What was that for?" she asks.

"That was just a warm up of things to come." She frowns. "What?"

"Tera just told me she's not going to be able to spend the night with the boys, so I'll have to come back here after the party."

I shrug. "I'm not seeing a problem here."

"I'm sure you'll want to go home and sleep in your own bed. My little bungalow is so small, squishy even."

"Are you that sure of me, Harper?" I ask, thinking after the last couple of weeks she might know me better than that. She eyes me and I give her another kiss. "I want to be in whatever bed you're in, and I don't care if it's my house or yours, okay?"

"Okay," she says with a soft sigh, her lips still poised, ready for more kisses. I brush my thumb over her plump bottom lip. Her eyes slowly open and she adds, "I'm going to be the designated driver tonight, because when we come back here to sleep, I have to be on high alert, in case one of the boys wake or gets sick or needs anything."

"No, you're not," I tell her, not needing alcohol as long as I have her by my side, and that is one messed up situation, because I only have her for a little while longer. She certainly made sure I knew that earlier. Why the hell does that bother me so much?

Oh, maybe because you want more, dude.

Oh shit, I want more.

HARPER

I take in Liam's profile as he drives back to Violet's house for Jason's party. My heart beats just a little faster in my chest, partly because the party animal just told me he's going to be the designated driver, and partly because I can't be photographed with him. I wasn't about to cause a scene at his place, but I didn't want him to skip the interview because I was uncomfortable. I mean, any publicity is good publicity for him, right? That gives me pause. Over the last couple of weeks, I saw a softer side to Liam Dalton. A caring, nurturing side that spoke of consideration for others, and not just for himself. The media paints him as a bad ass who cares little about rules, or others. I'm just not seeing that. Is it possible that he's not really a rule breaker, that he only does that because it's what's expected of him?

"You're awfully quiet," he says and lightly squeezes my arm, pulling my thoughts back.

"Are you sure you really want to do this?"

Hurt moves across his face. "Don't you think it's a little late to be second guessing this?" he asks as he pulls into the driveway. "But if you don't want me—"

"No, no, it's not that, Liam," I say and realize what he must be thinking. I straight up told him I didn't want to be photographed with him. I didn't tell him the reason why, and hopefully I never have to, but for a rule breaker who supposedly doesn't care about much other than hockey, partying and having fun, it's clear I hurt him on a deeper level. I just really don't want to get into my past, and what being seen with him could mean. "I want you."

"You want me?" he asks.

I laugh. "Well yes, I do, but I also want you to meet my friends. I think you're really going to like them."

"If they're friends of yours, then I'm sure I will." I bite my lip and exhale a groan. "What?" he asks.

"The guys are going to lose their minds when they meet you, and they'll want to talk hockey and monopolize your time when you're just trying to relax and—"

"I don't think we have anything to worry about." He gives me a playful wink as he kills the ignition. "I'm not their favorite, remember?"

I chuckle. "Yes, but I want you to have a nice time. It can't always be easy being 'on' for a crowd." I emphasize the word on, because deep down, I'm believing more and more that there are many more layers to this man.

"I can handle myself," he says to me.

"Later, if you play your cards right, I'd like to handle you too."

"Better yet, I get to handle you." He laughs and opens his door, but I like how he turned it around to wanting to touch me. It does the weirdest things to me, makes me feel special. Ridiculous, I know. I'm just one of many women. Or am I? "Do you need me to carry you?"

I roll my ankle. "Maybe later. It seems fine right now." I carefully exit the big ass truck, and Liam is right there on my side to catch me, but I don't fall. He takes the cake from me, and I shut the door. The soft thud carries in the quiet night.

"If I carry it in, do you think I can pass it off as mine."

"You can try, but everyone has tasted my lava cake already, so you'll have a hard time pulling it off. Actually, let me carry that, because the guys are going to lose their minds and I don't want you dropping this."

I take the cake from him and he puts his hand on the small of my back as we walk to the front door, and I like the way he's always touching me with such caring hands. I balance the cake and I'm about to knock when the door flies open. Violet's gaze goes back and forth between the two of us and a blush spreads across my face. Dammit, one look and she can tell we've been sleeping together. I haven't divulged that little secret yet, to her or Emma, but tonight, there's no hiding the truth and I expect an inquisition.

"Liam," she says. "It's so nice to finally meet you. Harper and Gavin have been keeping you all to themselves." She gives a playful wag of her brows. "I guess now I know why."

"Liam, this is Violet. My former best friend."

Liam laughs and shakes her hand. "Nice to meet you, Violet. I must confess though, it's me whose been keeping Harper and Gavin to myself. I'd like to say I'm sorry, but I'm not really."

Violet's very pleased dark eyes assess Liam as she steps back to make room for us to enter. Laughter comes from the other room, and I assume we're the last ones here for the dinner party. She nudges me, and gives me a scornful look, one filled with questions like: why didn't you tell me you were sleeping with him? I make a shushing sound, and we follow her to the kitchen.

"What can I get you guys to drink?"

"Soda for me," Liam says quickly, and Violet looks at him like he just sprouted a hockey stick from his head. "Designated driver," he explains.

"How thoughtful," she says. "Wine for you, Harper?"

I nod and she pours me a generous glass. "Okay, let's go meet everyone, and I apologize in advance, Liam."

We follow her to the living room, and I glance at Liam. "I feel bad that you're not drinking. Gavin is my responsibility, not yours."

"I don't need a drink to have a good time, and besides, I told you, I wanted to take care of you and Gavin. It's not just that I want to, Harper, I enjoy it."

My stupid heart does a little flip, but I don't have time to examine it when Jason tries to jump from his chair, and nearly topples backward. I mouth the words, "Smooth, Jason," when his gaze bobbles back and forth between Liam and me. I mean, he knew Liam was coming, but I guess seeing him up close and personal is a whole other ballgame, or should I say, hockey game.

"Liam," he finally says, the room full of couples falling silent as everyone gawks at Liam, and I don't blame them. He is kind of impressive. Why he's no one's favorite is beyond me.

"Nice to meet you, Jason," he says casually, and extends his arm. Jason hurries to him and they shake, and a few minutes later, after the introductions to Jason's brothers and their wives, and getting the hockey talk out of the way, Liam and I take a seat, and conversation turns to other things. I snuggle in next to him as both Violet and Emma stare at me, trying to get my attention so I'll slip into the other room and give the deets on our bedroom antics. But I tease them, pretend I don't notice them, but I did notice the hottie Emma is with. He really seems into her.

After torturing them long enough, I glance at Liam and say, "You'll be okay? I'm going to get a refill." He gives me a nod and smile and I head to the kitchen, and chuckle as Violet and Emma excuse themselves and come rushing in after me.

Violet skids to a halt. "Girlfriend, you've got some explaining to do."

"Who me?" I ask, all wide-eyed and innocent. "What on earth would I have to explain?"

"Just that you're tapping that, and didn't even think to tell us. Spill," Emma says, and pours more wine into her glass.

A bubble of excitement wells up inside me. "Yeah, I am tapping that." The girls hoot, and then quickly clamp their hands over their mouths when I hush them. "Good God, quiet down before Liam hears you."

"Everything." Emma holds her hand out, palm up and wiggles her fingers. "Now."

"It just sort of happened, over and over again," I say with a chuckle I can't contain, my heart light and full of giddiness.

"It's nice to see you happy, Harper." Violet gives me a big smile.

"You really like him, huh?" Emma says, and I don't miss the hint of worry wrapped around her words.

"He's really a nice guy, and yes, I like him. I wouldn't be sleeping with him if I didn't like him."

She angles her head, her lips thinning, and I get it. She thinks I've fallen for him and I haven't. I don't think. I hold my hands up. "Stop right now. This is just a hook-up. We decided to have a little fun together before he left for training."

"I think he really likes you too, Harper," Violet says.

"You do?" I ask far too quickly, because once again Emma is looking at me with concern all over her face. "Listen, you were the one who told me to turn my 'beaver-can't do', into a 'beaver-can do', Emma. Trust I know what I'm doing, okay?"

"Okay," she says, dropping it. She leans into me. "Are the rumors true?"

"What rumors?"

"You know..." She glances over her shoulder to ensure we're alone. "That he has a big, you know...stick."

Wine nearly comes out my nose as I laugh. "That, my friend, is not your business."

She sits back in her chair all smug like. "You don't need to answer. It's all over your face."

"Speaking about all over your face," Violet teases.

"Oh my God, stop," I shriek.

"What's all over whose face?" Jason asks, coming into the kitchen to grab some more beers. He takes one look at his wife's face and says, "Oh, never mind." We laugh as he grabs the beers and before he heads into the other room, he looks at me. "Liam is really nice, Harper. He's much different than I expected."

I nod, understanding exactly what he's saying. "Come on, let's get back in there."

We all head back to our seats and for the next couple of hours, we eat, drink and play charades, which Liam is surprisingly good at, even though he groaned and complained about having to play. He said he was good at it because he had loud sisters and had to find ways to be heard over them. I'm not sure if it's true or not, all I know is I really like this guy and haven't had this much fun in a long time, and I'd like to meet these sisters of his and hear about his childhood from their point of view, because I suspect they'd tell a completely different story. Not that I expect that to happen. We're hooking up only. No need to meet his family. But I continue to think about it until the time nears midnight. I dart into the kitchen to cut a couple slices of cake for Gavin and Holden, and afterward, Liam and I say our goodbyes at the door.

The night air falls over me, giving me a little chill as we hop back in the truck and head to my place. I have a stupid smile on my face I can't seem to shake.

"Fun night," Liam says, his mood mellow and soft, the atmosphere in the cab of his truck intimate and easy.

"I think everyone loved meeting you," I say, and what I don't say is that they were happy meeting 'him,' the real Liam. The one I'm lucky enough to get to know.

"You have great people in your life, Harper."

"You do too," I say, and think about Liam's birthday party. He said he doesn't want anything big, and while I know his friends are planning a huge get together, it does make me want to do something a little more private for him. I sink back into the seat as a plan forms.

"You look like you're up to something."

I turn my head. "Know me that well, do you?"

"I might."

I chuckle, so warm and content being with him. I reach across the seat and put my hand on his thigh. "Maybe there's something I want to get up."

"Already there," he says, and I shift my hand to find him half hard.

"Liam!"

He laughs. "What? I told you that kiss earlier was just a warm up, and I've not been able to stop thinking about getting my mouth on you."

A noise, a mixture between a mewl and moan slides from my lips. I love how much this guy wants me, worships me—in bed at least. Although is that really true? He's so good to me outside of the bedroom, taking care of Gavin, helping me at home and work.

A silence filled with sexual tension mushrooms inside the truck as he drives us home, and once we reach my place, he slams the vehicle into park and practically jumps from the cab. I laugh, loving his impatience.

"I have to pay the sitter and walk her home."

"I'll take care of that," he says, as I put my key in the door and unlock it.

"I'm quite capable."

"Your ankle, remember, plus you need to check on the boys and then get naked for me. I'm just speeding up the process."

"I had no idea you were such an efficiency expert, Liam."

"I'm a lot of things you don't know," he says, so quietly I spin, my gaze roaming his face. I think he's wrong about that. I know more than he realizes. I turn back and push open the door, and when I enter, I find Tera on the sofa, lost in a book. She stretches when she sees me, and her eyes go a bit wider when she spots Liam coming in behind me.

"Are you okay with Liam walking you home? If not, I will, no problem."

"That would be great," she says, a little star-struck as she looks at the infamous hockey player. She gathers her things and hurries outside with Liam. This will definitely give her something to talk about for years to come. I set the slices of cake on the kitchen counter, and hurry to Gavin's room. He and Holden are fast asleep in the bunk beds.

Deciding to have a quick shower, I make my way to the bathroom, turn the water on and strip off. I step into the hot spray and a moan crawls out of my throat, as I enjoy the glorious heat.

"Did you start without me?" My eyes widen at the sound of Liam's voice and I wipe the steam from the shower door to see that he's back already and a little out of breath.

"That was fast," I say as he locks the door.

"There's another word I don't like to hear when I'm getting naked with you," he teases. "But yeah, I walked Tera home and ran all the way back here." I laugh and my body tingles all over as he slides the door open and stands before me with a smile and an erection.

"Get your ass in here," I say, and grab his hand and tug. He steps in, closes the door, and turns me until my back is pressed against his chest. His hands slide around my stomach, and go higher until he's cupping my aching breasts. I lay my head on his shoulder as he teases my hard nipples and deep between my legs, I grow needy. "Liam," I murmur. God, will I ever get enough of this man? He's like an addiction I can't quit, which isn't a good thing. I pray when our time is over, he'll be out of my system.

"Need something?" he asks, his hot breath on my ear. I whimper, and he presses wet, open-mouthed kisses to my neck as one hand slides down, until it's between my quivering legs. I push forward, seeking his touch, and his groan of approval curls around me, stimulates me even more. He parts my damp lips with deft fingers, and a keening cry catches in my throat as he lightly strokes my clit.

"Such a needy, needy girl," he murmurs against my skin.

"Since it's all your fault, you're responsible for fixing it."

"I have no problem with that." He slides a thick finger into me, and I reach behind me, and put my hands on his hips as I move against his finger. He strokes me deep, and uses his palm to press against my clit. I close my eyes as pleasure grips my core.

"That is so good," I say, trying to keep my voice low, when all I want to do is scream his name. His finger moves a little faster, sliding in and out, the perfect pressure and rhythm to bring on a fast orgasm. "Liam," I cry out, as pleasure centers between my legs.

"Fuck, yeah," he growls as I clench around him, my hot juices spill down his hand as I let go. I sag against him, and he wraps one arm around my waist to hold me as he stays between my legs, his finger high inside me as I ride out the last delicious waves. I suck in a hard breath, needing to refill my lungs, and he pulls his finger from my sex and lightly pets me.

"That was fast," he says.

"Thought those were words you didn't like to hear when you were naked with me." His chuckle reverberates through me, and he spins me, his mouth finding mine. He kisses me deeply, passionately, once again stealing the breath from my lungs.

His beautifully hard cock presses against my stomach and I move my body, rubbing up against him until he's moaning into my mouth. I step back a bit, breaking his hold on me, and he angles his head.

"Get back...oh," he says, the word a little breathless whisper, as I take his hardness into my palms. I rub him, and dip into the pre-cum pooling on his crown to use it for lubrication. "Fuck, that's good, Harper."

I smile, and he shakes his head. "You love this, don't you?" he asks.

"I won't lie," I say. "I love getting naked with you."

He reaches out, and puts one hand on my neck, his face twisted in total agony as I stroke him. "You know what I mean."

"If you're asking if I love pleasuring you, the answer is yes," I say.

"You love torturing me, is more like it."

"Is this torture?" I run my hand along the length of him and take his balls into my hand, giving them a gentle squeeze. His hips come forward, pushing his cock against my hand and I say, "Okay, it's true, I do like watching you come unhinged."

I pull him from the spray and drop to my knees, taking him into my mouth and savoring the tangy taste of him. Widening my jaw to accommodate his impressive girth, I work to relax my throat and he jerks forward, like he wants to get his entire length into my mouth, but it's impossible.

"Harper, Jesus." His fingers tangle in my wet hair as he pushes it from my face to watch me take him in. "I love watching you take me like this." I glance up at him, catch the warmth mingling with lust in his eyes, and my heart squeezes tight. "Babe, if you keep it up, I'm going to come, and I want to be inside you for that."

I inch back and his cock sits on my bottom lip. "Can't we do both, because I really, really want you to come in my mouth, Liam."

His tortured growl fills me with want, and I grin, loving his reactions. "You can have both, babe. You can have whatever the fuck you want from me," he says, and that's when I realize two things, one he has no blood left in his brain—because he never would have put that out there—and two, it's quite possible I want everything with this man. The house, the fenced yard, the minivan filled with kids and a dog.

This is just sex, Harper.

But what if it's not?

I turn my focus back to his beautiful cock, and take him impossibly deeper, until he's in my throat and breathing is impossible, but I just don't care. I'm so goddamn wide open and lost in him, this moment, in pleasuring him, that I'll forgo air.

He tugs on my hair, but I won't let him drag me off. Nope, this man is going to release in my throat, no matter how much of a gentleman he's trying to be.

"Harper," he growls and I stay put, lodged between his legs. Not even his toughest linebacker could pull me off. No wait, that's football. Nevertheless, I'm not going anywhere. I massage his tight balls, and suck on him and a second later, his growl curls around me and fills me with bliss as he releases. He growls my name, and I swallow every drop I can. His beautiful cock is so hard and gorgeous as I inch back a bit and grip him with my palm. He's practically shaking and I sneak a peek to find him watching me, carefully.

Once he depletes himself, I go back on my heels and he growls. "Come here." He reaches down, and pulls me to my feet, sliding his arms around me and just holding me to him. I rest my face on his chest and revel in his strong heartbeat. A contented sigh crawls out of my throat, and I stifle a yawn.

"Don't think for a minute I'm letting you go to sleep," he says, and I laugh against him, snuggling impossibly closer. He positions me under the spray and we both rinse off. No words are spoken. A very beautiful, very comfortable silence envelopes us as he slides open the shower door, grabs a towel and wraps me in it. I'm so lethargic, I just stand there and watch as he dries off, gathers our clothes, and peeks out into the hall to make sure no little ones are up and running around.

His grin is so adorable when he turns back to me and says, "Coast is clear." I take a step toward him and frown. "What's wrong?"

"I don't have a spare room in this place. There is nowhere for you to sneak off to come morning."

"Yeah, I thought about that. I hate sneaking around." He scrubs his face, a frown on his forehead. "But we can't let Gavin get the wrong idea, right?"

I so want to tell him that I don't care, that I want more, but I'm too damn chickenshit to do it. "Maybe this isn't a good idea."

Sadness invades his eyes as his shoulders tighten. "Do you want me to go, Harper?"

"No," I say quickly. "I just..." God, how do I explain it, confess that I might just be falling for him? Maybe I should just blurt it out. I open my mouth, as he steps up to me, brushes the soft pad of his thumb over my cheek.

"How about this, I'll take you to bed, and in the middle of the night, I'll get up and sleep on the sofa."

"I can't ask—"

"All I want is a yes or no, Harper."

I take a deep breath, unable to watch this man walk out of my house tonight, especially with the way he's touching me, looking at me like I am a woman worthy of worship.

"Yes."

LIAM

I carry her to the bedroom and set her on her bed. I glance up, about to close her curtains, but I kind of like the way the moonlight slants against her wall and lights up the bed. She releases her towel in an inviting manner, and my cock once again hardens. I love that Harper isn't with me because I'm a hockey player, or using me for financial gain or status. She's a sweet and simple girl just trying to get by in life on her own merits, and would never sell photos of us to further her agenda.

"Are you ready for me again?" I ask. For some unknown reason I need to hear her say it.

"I'm ready," she says and lays back, her gorgeous body spread wide open, mine for the taking and dammit, I plan to take. Our mood is mellow, relaxed as I fish a condom from my pocket, tear into it, and quickly sheathe myself. Christ, the last time I needed to be inside a woman this bad was the last time I had Harper naked.

I slide between her damp legs, lightly pet her sex, and lean forward to press my lips to her hot clit. I give her a slow lick and her hips lift for me, just like I knew they would. I've never spent so much time with one woman in the past and I have to say I love getting to know her, love discovering all her little likes. She calls my name, and it's music to my ears as I slide up her body. With her feet flat, her knees bent, her legs fall open for me, and my cock slides inside her.

She gives a soft moan, and it mingles with my groan as I fill her core, banging against her cervix. She likes when I do that. It brings on a whole-body climax that leaves her shaken and me happy that I could do that for her.

My mouth finds hers and we kiss slowly, softly, our tongues playing gently as I move my hips, my cock inching in and out, in and out, until her slick juices coat me. Catching me by surprise, she pushes my chest, and for a second I think she's shoving me away until I realize from the heat in her eyes that she wants to ride me.

I roll to my back and pull her with me, until she's on top, her legs straddling my body, my dick high inside her. My hands span her waist and I lift her, helping her along as she moves against me, grinding hard as she seeks relief from my cock. I slide my hands up and take her tits into my palms.

"You are so beautiful."

She falls forward, presses soft kisses to my mouth, her hips still moving, still working my cock until she brings me right to the edge again. I slide my hand between our bodies and rub her wet clit with my thumb and she sits up right on my cock again. Her arms lift, and she takes her hair into her hands, looking like a magnificent piece of art as she fucks me.

Tiny spasms in her body wrap around my cock, and she grows slicker by the second. "That's it. Take what you need, babe."

"Liam..." she whispers softly, her eyes closed, her mouth open.

I take a couple of deep breaths as I lose myself in her just a tiny bit more. "I know, Harper, I know," I say, although I don't know anything at the moment, other than I could very well be in trouble where this woman is concerned.

She explodes around me, her hot release searing my dick, and dripping down my balls. "Fuck yeah," I say and change the pace, pounding into her a little harder. Her beautiful breasts bounce, and I delve deeper, hitting all the right spots until she's coming again, and I'm coming with her.

Her breath is coming in fast pants, matching mine as we both lose ourselves to the pleasure. I grip her hips and hold her still as the last of my orgasm takes hold. Her eyes open and the sweet grin on her face as her eyes meet mine, fucks me over just a little more.

"I am so glad you didn't want me to go," I say with a soft laugh.

She falls over me, and kisses me deeply. I grip her hair and brush it back over her shoulders. "Do you think you can stay in my bed for a little while longer?" she asks, and I resist the urge to tell her I'd be happy to stay forever because whatever she wants, she gets, and maybe this isn't all about her, because it's what I want too.

"Yeah," I say. "Let's just get cleaned up." I search her night-stand, find a box of tissues and remove my condom. I wipe between her legs and I'm about to slide in next to her, but a bang outside her house stops me in my tracks. "What the hell was that?" I ask.

Her eyes open wide, and fear washes the color from her face. "Harper?" What the hell? What would frighten her so badly.

"I don't know," she says. "It sounded like the garbage can."

"You stay here. I'll go check."

She reaches for me. "You don't need to go out there."

"It's fine." I scoop up my pants and shirt. "I'll check it out and be right back." I dress quickly as she ducks under the blankets and pulls them up to her neck. The bedroom door creaks open and I quietly head down the hall to the front door. Outside the night is quiet and dark, in the distance a dog can be heard barking, but there are no sounds coming from around Harper's place. She lives in a quiet, low-crime neighborhood so I'm assuming it was an animal or something.

When my search comes up empty, I head back into the house, lock the door, and tiptoe back to Harper's bedroom. She's in the exact same position as I left her. Her brows lift in question when I begin to strip, to crawl back into bed with her.

"I think it was an animal. Nothing out of the ordinary."

She nods quickly. "Okay, good."

"What did you think it was?" I ask as I slip in beside her and pull her close.

"An animal," she says quickly. I want to question her about it, because for the first time I get the sense she's not telling me the truth and that's not like her. But I decide to let it go and kiss the top of her head as she rests against my chest, and I briefly close my eyes, planning to stay here until she falls asleep and then make my way to her sofa. But sometimes the best laid plans....

The next thing I know I'm being awakened by footsteps running in the hall, and before I can get out of bed and get dressed, Gavin and Holden come running into the room.

Shit.

They both come to an abrupt halt when they see me in bed, and I glance at Harper to find her eyes wide with worry.

"Did you have a sleepover too?" Gavin asks.

I nod. "I did."

The boys look at us for a second, their innocent eyes taking in the scene before them, and then Gavin shrugs. "Want to play Fortnite with us?"

"You bet I do, buddy. You two go get it set up, and I'll be right out. We'll let your mom sleep in, and we'll eat cake for breakfast, okay?"

They both smile and high five each other before dashing from the room and once they're gone, Harper groans and puts the pillow over her head. I tug the pillow from Harper's face, and drop a kiss onto her head. "It's fine. They're kids, they don't know any better, and also I'm sorry, because I fell asleep. It was just so comfortable."

"What if they say something?"

"Who are they going to say something to, and does it really matter? We're consenting adults, doing what adults do."

"Yeah, but the papers."

"I'm sure Gavin isn't in the room calling any paparazzi," I tease.

"I know, but—"

"I promise you it's fine. Why don't you try to get a bit more sleep and I'll take care of the boys?"

She goes to push her covers off and I stop her. "You don't have to do that."

"I want to." I tuck her back in. "Also, how do you feel about a big homecooked Sunday dinner?"

"You're cooking it?"

"Hell no," I say quickly. "My folks love Sunday meals, and I thought it might be fun for Gavin. My sisters will be there, and their kids. I think he'd have a good time and I know they've been wanting to meet him."

"I don't want to impose." She rakes her teeth over her bottom lip. "Maybe you two should go, and I'll stay home."

"Not a chance. We're all going."

"I'll think about it, okay?"

"Okay," I say, conceding. "Get some sleep. I'm going to kick Gavin and Holden's ass at Fortnite." She grins at that, and I leave the room, instantly missing her presence, her touch, her smile. The boys are already in front of the TV as I make my way to the kitchen in search of coffee. I find the grounds, and put on a pot. As it brews, I search the drawers for a few forks and carry the cake to the boys.

"Yay, cake!" Gavin says and plunks down onto the sofa. I set the slices on the coffee table, and a thunk at the front door pulls my focus.

"What was that?"

"I dunno," Gavin says with a shrug as they both dive into their cake.

I walk to the front door, pull it open and find Sunday's newspaper on the stoop. I grab it and toss it onto the kitchen table as I grab a cup and fill it before the coffee maker beeps. As the boys chat and eat, I flip through the paper, and nearly spill my coffee when I come across the local entertainment section and see the photo of Harper and me.

"Shit," I grumble and glance over my shoulder. For a split second, I think about hiding it, but she'll likely hear about it from her friends sooner or later. This is the last thing Harper wanted but there we are, under the caption that says, House Broken. "Jesus." I scan the article, and it showcases Harper as a single mother dog walker, and leaves the reader wondering if the Rule Breaker has finally been broken.

"What's wrong?"

I turn to find Harper dressed in jeans and a T-shirt, standing in the archway staring at me. I exhale with a groan, and give the paper a shove. "You're not going to like this."

"Like what?" she asks and pushes off the door. She sees the paper on the table, and her face pales. "Liam...?"

"Sit." I pull a chair out and she drops into it. "Have your coffee first."

I snatch another mug from the cupboard, and cringe as she flips through the paper and I know the exact second she finds the article when a little whimpering sound reaches my ears.

"I'm sorry," I say. "I know you didn't want this."

"This picture," she says. "It's from the day we went to the ice cream shop."

"Yeah, I don't know how the paper got it." She scans the article, and her throat makes a noise as she swallows. I hand her the mug of coffee and she takes a much-needed sip.

I fall into the chair across from her. "It's not so bad, right? They didn't really say too much, other than I might be house broken."

She pushes the paper away. "It's bad. It's really bad."

I shimmy closer and take her trembling hand. "What's going on? Why is this so bad?"

"My ex," she says, and looks away, but not before I catch the worry in her eyes.

My muscles tighten. "Gavin's father?"

She shakes her head no, and I give her hand a little squeeze. "I...I was involved with a guy a few years back. I thought he was a good guy. He was there for me when Mom and Dad died, and Gavin was only one. I bought this house, and he moved in, and..."

"Did he hurt you?"

"Yes, no...sort of."

I take a big sip of coffee. My brain is going to need to be wide awake for this, I'm sure. "If he hurt you, Harper—"

"Devon's not a good guy. He was using me, and I didn't know until it was too late."

"Too late?"

"He drank, and gambled, fooled around on me, and you see...you..."

I nod, understanding completely. "You were afraid of bringing me into Gavin's life because of the drinking, and my reputation." It's not what she thinks, but right now this is about her, not me.

"Yeah, I couldn't go down that road again."

"What did he do?"

"I feel stupid."

"This is on him, not you. You were the victim obviously, and I'm not going to let you victim-shame yourself, Harper."

She nods. "Before I knew what was happening, he had drained my entire inheritance. I had been saving to open my own pet store and grooming business, and for Gavin's future, but he took it all, and he threatened my life, telling me he'd find me and kill me if I pressed charges or anything." She leans forward and presses her palms into her eyes. "I've been keeping a low profile, you know, and I'm worried that if he thought you and I were...you know..."

"Together," I say finishing her sentence, "Then he'd come sniffing around, looking for money."

"Something like that."

"Is he still in Seattle?"

"Liam, don't. I don't want you going after him or getting involved. I need you to promise me that."

I take a few fast breaths. "Where does he live?"

"I don't know."

"Where does he work?"

Her face is unsure when she glances at me. "I won't go after him unless he gives me reason, okay?"

"He's a mechanic. Randy's Auto Repairs, South Seattle."

I know the place, and I store that information away just in case. "I won't let him hurt you, Harper. I won't let him hurt Gavin either, and I'm not going to say his threat against you was simply a scare tactic, but a guy like that sounds like a total coward, and would be too afraid to come around if you were with me. Men like that bully women, not other guys."

"You're not always going to be around, Liam," she tells me, her body stiffening, and fuck, she's right. I have a hockey career that takes me on the road, but deep inside what she's saying goes deeper than that. She's letting me know this thing between us is only temporary.

"I know," I say. "Let's hope you're worried for nothing. Maybe he won't even see this. It's not even on the front page."

She nods, but I don't get the sense she believes that, and I guess she does know him better than me. "I just don't trust him." She lifts a shaky hand and waves it back and forth between the two of us. "Maybe I never should have...I mean, I don't want to make my problems yours."

Hurt and anger and protectiveness all hit at once. I fucking want her problems to be mine. I want to be there for her, but it doesn't seem like she wants the same. Goddammit, I need to change her mind about that somehow.

My fingers fist and I work to keep the anger pinging around inside me like a runaway pinball in check, when all I want to do is go out and beat the shit out of the guy. I almost snort at that. Wouldn't a beatdown do wonders for my career and endorsements. Fans would probably expect it, cheer me on, but my coach would kick my ass and I could kiss my endorsements goodbye. I'd still do it, though. If that fucker comes around, I'm going to be having a long-ass talk to him—with my fists.

I pull her onto my lap, and wrap my arms around her, cocooning her in my strength. She gives me a shaky smile. "Maybe you're right. Maybe I've just built this up in my head."

I consider the noise we heard outside last night and my stomach tightens. But this article didn't come out until this morning. If someone was banging around outside the house, it couldn't have been him, right?

Unless...unless it was.

12

HARPER

I have no idea why my stomach is in knots or why I'm so damn nervous. I'm a grown woman, meeting a friend's family. A friend with benefits, but a friend nonetheless. Still, it's not like I'm his girlfriend, and I'll be under scrutiny from all his sisters. I'm being ridiculous and I know it. Unless they can tell that we have sex written all over us.

"I should have made something," I say, and fold my hands on my lap.

"They don't expect me to bring anything." He chuckles quietly. "Not any more anyway."

I study his strong profile as he drives through downtown. "What's that mean?"

"They once asked me to make squash, and I cooked it until it was a sacrificial offering." We both laugh at that and he adds, "I set the bar really low, so now they don't ask."

"Yeah, but I'm not you, and I should have brought more than a store-bought baguette. I should have made a lava cake."

"Hell no. That sets the bar too high, and then every time you came, they'd expect it."

"It's not like I'm ever going to have dinner with them again, Liam," I say, reminding him of our timeline. Oh, and why is that? Because I want him to tell me the hell with it, that we don't have to end this when summer is over? Yup, that's pretty much it.

I smooth my hand over my summery dress and take a look at Gavin in the back seat. He's been so happy these last couple weeks, hanging out with Liam, and doing so many fun things. My heart squeezes tight as I listen to him singing out loud. He really needed a man in his life. A good man, like Liam. Not a man like my ex. An uneasy quiver goes through me. I really hope he doesn't come sniffing around, now that he knows a famous hockey player is in our lives. I'm not sure what he thinks he could get out of it, but I wouldn't put anything past him.

I go quiet, lost in thought, and a short while later, he pulls into his parents' driveway. I glance at the older home in an older neighborhood. With its manicured lawn, and landscaping, it's very quaint and inviting. "You grew up here."

"Yup." He winks at me. "Want to see my bedroom?"

"I do. I want to see it," Gavin pipes up and I shake my head. Even when I don't think he's listening, he's listening.

"You bet, buddy."

We all exit his big truck and head up the three steps to the front door. He pushes it open and says, "Your favorite son is home." That makes me laugh, considering he's the only son. When no one answers, he says, "They must all be out back."

"I can't believe they weren't all waiting at the door with balloons and a parade for their favorite son."

"Where's the love?" he teases. "Come on." We walk through the house, and I slow, looking at the pictures littering the walls. "Look at this one, Gavin. Liam doesn't have any front teeth."

"Adorable then, adorable now. I know, I know," he says as Gavin laughs at the picture, and as he touches his own front teeth. Warmth fills my heart, but the pictures make me miss my own family.

"Excuse me," he says to his family as he steps out back. "Where is all my fanfare?" he spreads his arms, and his family just laughs at his antics, but his behavior is different here. He's being himself, not showing off for the crowd or camera, and I have to say I like the real Liam. A lot.

He turns and winks at me, before taking Gavin's hand and putting his big palm on the small of my back to push me a little bit ahead of him.

"This is Harper, and my little brother, Gavin."

"Hi everyone," I say with a smile and take in the big backyard, the barbecue, the adults around a table and the kids with their fathers playing a game of ring toss. My heart pinches, and a wave of emotions roll through me. Visions of my parents flash in my mind. I miss them so damn much. Miss this kind of family gathering. I take a breath, and get the sense Liam understands my headspace as he steps closer.

"Gavin, do you want to play ring toss with everyone?" Gavin nods, and Liam calls over one of the boys around Gavin's age. "Gavin, this is Josh. Josh, why don't you take Gavin to play with you, and I'll be right over."

"Okay," he says and the two run off to play with the other kids. One of the women at the table stands and pulls a chair out for me.

"Come have a seat, Harper."

"Thanks." I drop down into the chair. The next thing I know, a glass of wine is in front of me, and Liam does the introductions. I say hello to his three sisters, and his folks, and wave to the guys playing with the kids, and I instantly feel comfortable with them all. I have no idea what I was worried about. They're all so nice and inviting.

Liam touches my hand, and angles his head in question when I pull it away and tuck it into my lap. "You okay if I go play with the kids?"

"Sure, go ahead," I say as he looks at me for a second longer before he goes off to hang with his brothers-in-law and nieces and nephews.

"Your son is adorable," Liam's sister, Tanya, says as I watch the kids playing. "That one is mine." She points to the little girl around six. She's standing over the boys with her hands on her hips, and she reminds me of Daisy and her take-no-crap nature. What was Tanya's daughter's name again? Robyne, right. "Robyne is such a pretty name."

Her eyes go wide and her head goes back. "What?"

I glance around, to find all eyes at the table on me. "Did I get her name wrong?"

"No, it's just surprising that you know my daughter's name." She runs her finger around the rim of her wine glass, her gaze moving over my face, and I wonder what it is she's seeing... thinking. I'm not sure, but whatever it is, it's putting a big smile on her face.

"Well, yeah, Liam filled me in." I hold my hand out and start checking off the names with my fingers. "There's Robyne, Josh, Jax, and Melody."

"Isn't that interesting," Krista says and reaches for the wine glass to give everyone a refill. "I didn't think he talked about us to his girlfriends, and he's certainly never brought one home to meet us before."

He's never brought a girl home before?

"Oh, no. I'm not his girlfriend or anything. He's Gavin's big brother from the organization, and I'm just Gavin's mother."

"Gavin's mother who he gave an old pair of my skates to," Krista says. "He's never done that before."

"Thank you for letting me borrow them," I say. "I'm not much of a skater, though."

"I can see why he's been keeping you to himself, though," Tanya says, a coy grin on her face. "I guess we can cut him some slack, now that we know why he's not been around."

I give a fast shake of my head. "He's not been keeping me to himself. It's just I sprained my ankle and he felt responsible and it wasn't his fault, but he insisted Gavin and I stay at his place, and he's been trying to help me out. That's probably why he hasn't been around." Oh, God, why am I rambling? All eyes continue to stare, and I take a big drink of wine to stop myself from saying anything more.

"You and Gavin are staying at his place?" Bethany asks as she shifts Jax in her arms. The question is innocent enough, but there's genuine shock in her eyes.

"Well, we were, but last night my friend had a party, and my sitter..." I take a breath. "I didn't stay there last night. My ankle is feeling much better." Heck, it was feeling better ages ago, but they don't need to know that, nor do they need to know Liam stayed at my place with me, and I might have fallen a little more in love with him.

"Girls, what did I tell you about interrogating our guests?" his dad, Ben, says with a laugh.

"We're not interrogating," Tanya says, and gives a little dismissive wave with her hands. "We're just getting to know Liam's girlfriend, is all."

"I'm not his girlfriend," I say. Why the heck are they not listening to me?

His mother, Sandra, with the same dark eyes as Liam, leans across the table and puts her hand on mine. "Of course you're not, dear." I glance at her, and even though she's agreeing with me, there's a look of disbelief in her eyes. "So, what do you do, Harper?"

Now that we're on a more comfortable topic, I say, "I work at Petco, and I have a dog walking service." I laugh quietly as I think back to when Liam helped me and got all tangled up in the leashes. "I'm hoping to someday open my own business."

"Ohmigod you're perfect," Bethany says, and I glance at her, not knowing what she means.

"Perfect?"

Just then the guys all finish playing, and come back to the table and Ben announces that the steaks are ready. Liam glances around the table and points to his sisters, one by one. "You girls had better not be making up lies about me."

"We weren't," Tanya says. "Getting to know Harper was much more interesting than talking about you."

"What's to tell, anyway? You were a book worm, and rarely came out of your room."

"Where's the love?" he says with a laugh. "And I never came out of my room because you three tortured me." He glances at me. "They dressed me up. Even put makeup on me. We didn't need a pet." He pokes his chest. "I was the pet."

As everyone laughs, and totally agrees with him, Jax starts fussing in Bethany's arms. She hands her son to Liam. "Hold him for a minute, will you. I have to go make up his bottle." Liam takes him into his arms and when he smiles down at him, my damn ovaries clench.

"Who's your favorite uncle?" he asks him, and he coos as he wraps his small fingers around Liam's.

"You're my favorite uncle," Robyne says, and turns to Gavin. "Is Uncle Liam your uncle or your Daddy?"

A groan catches in my throat, and I quickly say, "No he's not Gavin's uncle or daddy." As soon as the words leave my mouth, Liam's gaze jerks to mine. "He's Gavin's big brother, of sorts. What that means is that Liam hangs out with him."

"Where's Gavin's daddy?" she asks, and a sweat breaks out on my body. God, I do not want to get into my personal life with Liam's family.

Gavin blinks up at me. "Mommy, where's my daddy?"

"If he doesn't have a daddy, then Uncle Liam can be his daddy." Robyne puts one hand on her hip and has a look on her face like she just solved all the world's biggest problems.

Liam's mom reaches for Robyne's hand. "Sweetie, why don't you come and sit next to me?" Robyne smiles and hops away, and I take Gavin's hand.

"Do you want to sit by me?" He looks like he's about to press the daddy issue and I say, "I think they have soda pop." His eyes go wide, and I meet Liam's glance and wince. Great parenting moment, I know.

"Nice save," he says quietly, but there's something in his eyes, a sadness of sorts.

Bethany comes back out and after missing that very awkward moment, puts her hand on her brother's arm and says, "Look how good you are with him. When are you going to get married and give us a niece or nephew to spoil?"

Liam hands Jax back. "Don't start with that," he says and glances at me. "Three sisters and not one brother. What did I ever do to deserve that?" he asks, and the mood around the table lightens.

We all sit down to eat, and the food is delicious, conversation is fun and light and we all laugh over childhood stories and there is so much love at the table, it overflows in my heart. Beneath the table, I give Liam's leg a squeeze and smile at him when he looks my way. Once the meal is done, I sit back in my chair, sure I've never been so full in my life.

"So, what do you say, Gavin? Want to see my room?"

Gavin nods, and Tanya puts both hands on the table, palms down. "Up to your old tricks again, I see."

A goofy grin crosses his face when he says, "What?"

She glares at him, then turns to me. "This is what we call pulling a Liam."

"What does that mean?" I ask, loving the comradery between siblings and hating that Gavin is growing up without a brother or a sister. I've just been too afraid, but Liam...he doesn't make me afraid, which should frighten me all the more if he's not into me like I'm into him.

"He always had a reason to leave before the dishes were done. He'd make an excuse and slip off to his room to read."

"I'm beginning to think you were a book nerd, Liam," I say, and he gives me a look, like he's trying to gauge how I feel about that. "Not that there is anything wrong with that. I grew up on a farm, not too many kids around, and I lost myself in books all the time."

"Go," Sandra says, and points to the patio door. "Go show Gavin and Harper your shrine."

He laughs. "It's only a shrine because you don't want to change it."

She laughs, a look of pride on her pretty face. "He might be right about that."

"I can help with the dishes," I tell her.

"Your first time here, you're a guest. The second time, we'll put you to work in the kitchen," she says with a laugh and as I look at her, and all his family, I can't help but want to be a part of it and get put to work in the kitchen.

Oh, Harper, why did you have to go and fall for the rule breaker?

LIAM

I check my phone, and it's insane how much disappointment sits in my gut when I see Harper hasn't texted me. Yeah, sure, I'm out with the guys—they wanted to get together for a drink to celebrate my upcoming birthday—sitting at Nelly's pub, enjoying a couple beers and a few rounds of pool, but the truth is, while I love my team, I really want to be with Harper. She's become something of an addiction I don't want to—can't—quit. A smile I have no control over spreads across my face, and Cole nudges me with the pool cue.

"If you're done making out with your phone, it's your turn."

I tuck my phone away, grab my cue, and take a shot. The ball bounces off the side, and slides into the corner pocket.

"Lucky shot," my buddy Zander says as he gestures for the waitress. The guys are all enjoying the last days of summer before we all take off for training. They've invited me along, and wanted me to bring Harper and Gavin, but I'm not sure. I kind of like our quiet time at home.

Home.

For the first time, my big old place feels like a home, with Harper and Gavin filling the silence with laughter and fun. I take another shot and miss, and walk back to Cole. I snatch up my beer and glance around, noticing our audience as I take a long pull. Cason comes from the hallway, and I laugh as he gets stopped a million times. He signs autographs and smiles as his fans take their picture with him. Deciding I too need a trip to the little boys' room, I set my beer down, pull my hat lower on my head, not that people aren't going to recognize me, and move past Cason as he charms his fans.

I push open the bathroom door and some guy follows in behind me. I unzip and go about my business, trying not to fidget as the guy stands beside me, close, attending to his own business. I finish up, and make my way to the sink.

"You're Dalton, right?" he asks, using my last name.

"That's me," I say and flash him a bright smile, even though I don't feel like being 'on' right now.

"The one they call the rule breaker."

"Right again."

I wash my hands, and he steps up to the sink beside me. "I saw you in the paper the other day."

I slowly angle my head, and assess the guy beside me. An uneasy feeling prowls through my blood. "Yeah, I was in the paper."

"The girl you were with." He snickers. "She's not your usual type, huh?"

I pull myself up to my full height, and wipe my hands. "She's a friend," I say.

Under his breath, he says, "I bet she is."

I shift to face him straight on. "Do you have something to say?"

"Hell no," he says and puts his hands up, palms out. "Just saying…"

"What exactly are you saying?" I ask, as I square off against him, the bathroom door opens and in walks Alek. He takes one look at us, and without question moves in beside me.

"Who's your friend?" Alek asks.

"Didn't get that far in conversation yet."

The guy gives us a greasy grin, and swipes his hand through his hair. "The name's Griff," he says. "I'm a big fan."

"Nice to hear that," Alek says.

An awkward silence falls over us, and Griff grins, like he knows something I don't, and my fingers curl into fists at my sides, wanting to punch it from his face. "I guess I'll be going. Don't want to keep the missus waiting," Griff says and walks around us. I turn to Alek, take in his questioning eyes.

"What the hell was that all about?"

I shrug my tight shoulders. "Beats me, but I don't get a good feeling from the guy."

Alek puts his hand on my shoulder, and pulls it back quickly. "Whoa buddy, you need to relax."

I exhale. "Yeah," I say and pull my phone from my pocket when he steps away. I check for messages from Harper. She had to walk the dogs earlier and I thought she'd be back by now. I shoot her off a text, and try to shake the uneasy feeling mushrooming inside me. That guy clearly got under my skin when he mentioned Harper.

I step from the bathroom, and before I realize what's happening, some girl jumps on me, wrapping her legs around my back and pressing her mouth to mine.

What the fuck?

I put my arms around her, and try to get her off as she thrusts her tongue into my mouth, but can't shake her so easily. I finally manage to wiggle her from my body, and she gives me a big smile. "Do I know you?" I ask. Yeah, okay, I'm used to girls hitting on me, we all are, but getting accosted in a hallway isn't something that happens every day.

"No, but you can get to know me, if you want to." The scent of her floral perfume clouds the air and almost gags me. "I don't live far from here."

"I'm seeing someone," I say. I mean it's the truth. I am seeing Harper, sort of, and when it comes down to it, I'm a one-woman kind of guy.

She twirls her hair in her fingers, and sticks her chest out. "She never has to know."

"Yeah, well, I'd know, and I'm not a cheater."

She gives a big humorless laugh, the heat in her eyes turning venomous. I guess she's a woman who's used to getting her own way. In the past I would have taken her up on her offer. Would have fucked her ten ways to Sunday—I had to keep the fans happy and my reputation intact right—and go home with a little less of my soul. Damn, that seems like a lifetime ago. Over the last month, my priorities have shifted, all thanks to Harper and Gavin.

"That's not what I hear," she challenges.

What she hears and what's true are two different things. Alek comes from the bathroom, and once again goes still. I take that moment to get away. "If you'll excuse us." She glares at me as Alek and I move past her.

"What's going on with you tonight?" Alek asks.

"Beats me." My phone pings and I smile when I see it's from Harper.

"Maybe you should call it a night, buddy. Seems like you're rather distracted."

"Yeah, okay," I say. "I think I'll get out of here." I head over to the guys and naturally they call me all kinds of names when I tell them I'm cutting out early, but who are they to talk? Most of them are married with kids now, and were once where I am right now.

And where is that, Liam?

Oh, just falling for a girl I probably shouldn't be falling for, a girl who isn't looking for long term.

Fuck me.

I head toward the door, and as an uneasy feeling once again moves through me, I scan the bar, and find Griff's eyes on me, that same greasy smile on his face. The sudden need to get to Harper grips me, and I hurry outside and jump in my truck. Twenty minutes later, I'm at my place, and when I walk inside and hear music, my nerves settle.

I head to the kitchen, and find her swaying to the music coming from the other room as she stands before the microwave, popcorn bursting in the bag inside. I take her in, admiring her body in her pajama T-shirt and matching pink shorts. Her hair is damp, either from a shower or a swim. I have never seen her look hotter, or more adorable in my life. I am in so much fucking trouble here. My gaze moves to the patio door, which is slightly cracked, a warm night breeze blowing in.

"Hey," I say, not wanting to scare her.

She spins and the second my eyes meet hers, and I see the smile on her face, my heart squeezes tight.

She blinks up at me, her body warm, soft, beckoning mine, and I fall just a little harder for her. Fuck, man, I have to tell her, but what if she doesn't want the same things. What if I ruin this last week between us?

What if I don't?

"What are you doing home so early?" she asks, a little breathless, and I chalk it up to her arousal matching mine.

I take three big steps and close the distance between us. "Not happy to see me?"

She puts her arms around my neck, like it's the most natural thing in the world, and I hope to hell she doesn't smell that other girl's perfume on me. There's no sense in bringing it up. Nothing happened. Then again would she care? We're not a couple. Not committed. We're just fucking, right? I mean she can see other guys if she wants. Of course, that would have to be over my dead body.

"Sure I am, but I don't want to keep you from your friends."

"I had a drink, played some pool, but I'd much rather be here with you." Unable to help myself, I press my lips to hers and every nerve in my body comes alive. I growl into her mouth as I devour her, never able to get enough. The microwave beeps and pulls me back. "Is Gavin asleep?" I ask when I break the kiss, leaving us both needy and breathless.

"He's actually staying at Holden's tonight. Violet brought Holden for a swim, and then she took Gavin back to her place." She crinkles her nose. "I hope you don't mind that I invited my friend for a swim. I would have texted and asked first, but I didn't want to interfere."

"You're never interfering, Harper, and you never have to ask permission. My house is your house."

She gives me a playful smile. "Speaking of this big house, we have it all to ourselves tonight."

"So, what you're really saying is that I can strip you naked, lay you across the island and feast on you until sunup."

A fine quiver goes through her, and her pupils dilate, and I love that she likes the sound of that plan as much as I do. She moves around me, and backs up, a sexy, come hither look on her face. "I'm sure glad you came home early," she says as she grips the island and lifts herself up. She widens her legs in invitation. "Why are you so far away?"

Loving this playful mood she's in, I grip her thighs, spread them more, and insert myself in between. "Close enough?" I ask.

"Nope," she says, and reaches over my back to tug on my T-shirt. She drags it over my head and I help her, tearing it from my body, needing skin on skin sooner rather than later. Her eyes travel the length of me, and I must say, I do love the appreciation in her eyes when she looks at me. Her soft hands graze my body, and I groan as her warm fingers spread wide, touching me all over, like it's the first time she's ever explored my body. Honest to God, sex has never been this good with any woman.

I lean into her, breathe in her sweet, fruity scent. "Fuck, that feels good."

"Still not close enough," she murmurs as my hands span her waist, and I find her braless beneath her T-shirt. She arches into my touch and her little moan of pleasure strokes my cock.

"I like coming home to this," I say. "A guy could get used to it."

She wets her bottom lip, and I slide my hands under her shirt to cup her gorgeous, full breasts. I massage gently, and bury my mouth in the crook of her neck. I press hot, wet kisses to the spot that makes her insane, and her nails scrape my skin.

I inch back, take in the flush on her cheeks as I peel her shirt from her body. My gaze drops to her hard nipples. "You're perfect, Harper," I say. "So goddamn perfect."

"You're not so bad yourself, Liam. There is one little problem, though."

"Little?" I ask teasingly. "That's one of those words I don't like to hear when I'm getting naked." Her soft chuckle curls around me, seeps under my skin and beats against my pounding heart. I fucking love seeing her this happy. Hell, I want to make her this happy every day of the year.

"Our little problem is you're overdressed." She waves her finger up and down my body, and if there was a world record for getting naked, I would have just broken it.

"That's much better," she says, her teeth raking her lower lip as her gaze drops to my raging hard cock. "Now get over here, you're too far away."

I step into her. "Close enough?"

"No," she says and reaches down to take my cock into her soft palms. She strokes me from base to crown, and I power my hips forward, wanting more, everything. "I think I might want this in my mouth," she says, so demure like I nearly lose it. I fucking love everything about this woman.

"Me first," I say as she wiggles her ass on the countertop, which I'll never be able to look at again without thinking about fucking her on it. I grip her pajama shorts. "Lift for me."

She braces her hands on the counter, and lifts. I tug on her shorts, drag them down her legs and toss them away. "That's way better." I widen her legs again, and her dampness glistens in the overhead light. I run my hands up her thighs, and she goes back on her arms, opening herself to me, and I lick her, taste her sweet arousal with the soft blade of my tongue.

"Liam," she cries out, and moves her body, writhing against my invading tongue. I slide a finger into her tight core, and small little tremors tug at me. I can't believe she's already so close.

She falls back onto the counter, her breathing heavy and labored. I lift her legs, put them around my neck and slide my hands under her sweet ass. I lift her to my mouth, and feast on her as she grips the edges of the counter, and bucks against my face. Jesus, I love giving her this kind of pleasure.

I eat at her, fuck her with my tongue, my cock so goddamn hard, it's ready to drill through the side of my kitchen island. Her sweet pussy rocks against my mouth and I bury my face in deeper, until she's coming all over me, soaking my face, and dripping down my chin. I fucking love it.

"Liam," she calls out and I glance up to take in the way her head is going from side to side, her hair a tangled mess beneath her and come to the fast realization that she's never looked more beautiful.

When she stops spasming, I break from between her legs, and she goes up on her hands, her eyes dazed, a small smile tugging at the corners of her mouth. I pull her to me, and she wraps her legs around my body as I pull a chair from the table and settle on it.

As she sits on my lap, her breasts before my mouth, I take one nipple between my teeth and gently clamp down. "I'm going to need to fuck these soon," I say, and she wiggles against me, her hot pussy soaking my thighs.

"Liam," she says, and I glance up at her, take pleasure in the aroused look on her face. A look I put there, and if she agrees, I'll continue to put there long after our summer ends. Fuck, I'd like nothing better than to keep her here forever, for her and Gavin and maybe even a few more kids to fill my house with love and laughter long after our agreed-upon hook-up ends. For the first time in my grown life, I'm not afraid to be myself, not afraid someone won't like the guy I am. Harper has given me the gift of being myself, of liking that guy I am with her. More importantly, I'm pretty sure she likes that guy too.

"Yeah?"

"Not close enough."

Knowing exactly what she's saying and what she wants—what I want too—I lift her, and hold her over my raging erection.

She squirms, trying to get on me, but I lower her gently, offering one inch at a time, until her eyes are rolling back in her head. Once I'm seated high, I put my hands around her, holding her down.

"Close enough?" I ask, reveling in the feel of her against my body.

"Finally," she says with a little breathless sigh and rakes her hands through my hair, tugging gently to pull my head back, my mouth open. Her lips meet mine, and our tongues play and tangle as we both sit there, not moving as we simply enjoy my cock high inside her body. It's strange really, just to be sitting idle like this, buried inside her, but it's also perfect, like we're both finally at peace, existing as one, like it completes us.

I run my hands down her back, and we explore one another, touching, tasting, and teasing. Soon enough she begins to rock her hips, slowly, gently, twirling my cock inside her tight body. she sits up a little straighter, takes one of her breasts in her hands and feeds it to me. I lap at her, swirl my tongue around her peaked nipples, until her head falls back, my name on her tongue.

I move with her, sliding my cock in and out, until nothing exists but the two of us. We cling to each other, both taking and giving, and soon enough she's coming all over my cock again. I suck in air as her heat scorches me, and when I finally deplete myself, I cup her face, bring it to mine and press soft kisses to her mouth. I need to tell her. I need to confess, tell her that I've fallen for her. I open my mouth about to do just that, but slam it shut again when her eyes go wide, like she's just witnessed a car wreck.

"Harper?

HARPER

"Liam," I say. "We didn't use a condom."

"Shit." He grabs a fistful of hair and tugs. "I can't believe I forgot." I take in the worry in his eyes as he gazes at me, and I'm pretty sure I have the identical look on my face. It's clear he doesn't want children, and heck, I don't either. Well, that's not entirely true. I do want children, just not outside of marriage again. He takes my face in his hands. "I'm clean, Harper. I don't have sex without protection. I promise."

"I believe you," I say, and I do. He has no reason to lie to me, and from everything I've seen in Liam, he's a good man.

His eyes narrow. "But pregnancy. Are you on the pill?"

I shake my head, kicking myself for not getting on the pill when we agreed to this hook-up. "I'm not. I haven't been with anyone in a very long time," I admit, but get the sense that he knows that anyway.

"Is that morning after pill really a thing?" He shakes his head. "Sorry for being stupid."

"You're not stupid. If you always used protection, you had no need to think about a morning after pill."

He tugs on his hair. "I can't believe I forgot."

"I forgot too." I search his face, and I swear I've never seen him look more vulnerable than he does right now. "I think we're okay. I know where I am in my cycle and I was a bit crampy earlier today. But I can look into that tomorrow, if you want me to."

He looks down, and I can almost hear the wheels turning in his busy brain. "I don't..." His gaze lifts, and he exhales. "It won't make you sick or anything, will it?"

I smile, loving his concern for me. "No, I'm sure I'll be fine."

He snorts and shakes his head, his eyes wide, incredulous. "Can you imagine if we got pregnant."

Actually, yes I can.

"Nope, can't imagine," I say as he gazes at me, and for the briefest of seconds, I think he might actually like the idea. "Want to go for a swim?" I ask, needing a moment to get myself together, because suddenly the thoughts of having this man's child, of us all being a family, floods my system with emotions that frighten me a little. It's been a long time since I put myself out there, or wanted to. Liam made it so damn easy, and while I trust him—I really do believe he's more than the rule breaker—I'm not one hundred percent sure we want the same thing. While a part of me wants to ask, there is another part of me that's too afraid. What if I ruin our last week together, and while we agreed not to let this come between him and Gavin, what if it does? What if I was the reason he walks out of Gavin's life? My God, I'd never forgive myself.

"Sure, sounds good."

"I'll go get my suit," I say, and lift myself. He slides out of me, and tingling sensations race through my body.

He captures my arm before I can flee. "Forget the suit. The backyard is private."

"Okay," I say, and he stands, grabs a few tissues to wipe us clean and I try to ignore my pounding heart as we head out to the backyard. The moon is full, lighting up the pool as we both slide in. The cool water slides over my skin, and I dunk to freeze my thoughts, and ice my emotions.

When I surface, Liam is right there, pulling me into his arms. His lips find mine, and he kisses me slowly, like we have all the time in the world, but we don't. We only have until next weekend, and then he leaves, but it's going to be one hell of a weekend, and maybe that will just have to be enough for me, because every day of the week I'd forgo my own happiness for my son's.

We stand there with our arms around one another, and I put my head on his chest. His strong heart pounds against my cheek as he goes quiet, thoughtful. He finally breaks the quiet of the night.

"Harper."

"Yeah?" I lift my head, meeting his eyes.

His throat works as he swallows. "I wouldn't abandon you if you were pregnant," he says so quietly I have to strain to hear.

"I know, Liam. But I think we're okay."

"I...we...yeah, okay," he says and I have the feeling there is more he wants to say. That's when another thought hits, and my stomach sours.

"You know I would never get pregnant on purpose, right? Like to trap you or something. I know things like that can happen to professional hockey players, and well, to lots of guys."

He gives a fast shake of his head. "I trust you, Harper." He blows out a breath. "I don't really trust too many people," he says. I go quiet and wait for him to continue. "I guess you know what happened, right?"

I run my finger over his jaw. "If you're talking about the video, I didn't see it. I didn't want to see it."

"I appreciate that." He races his big hands up and down my arms, creating heat.

I snuggle in tighter, put my arms around his wide back. "Why did she do it, anyway?"

"She wanted more. I didn't. I guess it was a combination of revenge and money." He snorts, a sound of disgust in his throat. "She got paid big bucks from Dirt. I didn't even know she was recording us."

"You didn't?"

"Hell no. Sex is private to me."

"It is to me too, and what she did was disgusting." A noise sounds in the bushes, and we both turn. "What was that?"

"I don't know, probably an animal. Let's go inside, you're starting to shiver."

We climb from the pool, and head inside. After we dry off, we both tug on a pair of his sweats and I put on my pajama T-shirt, while he grabs a clean shirt from his dresser. Ten minutes later, with a bowl full of popcorn, we sit on his sofa and I turn on a chick flick. He groans, but there's a small smile on his face.

I throw a piece of popcorn at him. "Oh, come on. You can stop pretending you don't like it."

He laughs and pulls me to him. "I admit to nothing."

"Did your sisters make you watch?"

He arches his brow. "Are you trying to make me cash in my man card?" I laugh at that and snuggle in closer. He goes quiet for a very long time, and I stare at the TV, but I'm so lost in Liam, his warm scent, and his mere presence over-whelming me, that it's hard to concentrate on anything. "Harper?"

"Yeah."

"I like sleeping with you."

I angle my head to see him and he has a strange almost tortured look on his face. "I like sleeping with you too."

He scrubs his face, the way he always does when he's think-ing. I smile at that, realizing I know a lot about him and what makes him tick. "What I'm trying to say is...well, you said you haven't been with anyone in a long time. I'm glad you broke that dry-spell, or whatever you want to call it, with me."

"You're glad I chose you as my big daddy?" I tease.

He smiles. "Something like that."

"What can I say, Liam. You're a big fat snack. No girl can resist that."

This time he laughs out loud. "I've been called many things, but a big fat snack was never one of them."

I grin up at him, loving how easy he is to be with, how different he is with me behind closed doors. My phone pings from the other room, and I sit up. "I should grab that."

"Sure," he says, his brows pulling together. "Everything okay?"

"Yeah, it might have something to do with work," I fib. But I can't tell him what I've been up to. It's a surprise. I hurry to the kitchen, and check my messages, and almost do a fist pump when I see that I can get next weekend's shift covered. I really need the money, but I want to do something special for Liam and if it means working longer and harder after he leaves so I can finally start my own business, so be it. I send back a thank you to Becca, who agreed to cover for me, and I walk back into the room to find Liam leaning watching me.

"All good?" he asks.

I shrug it off. "Yeah, it was just a work thing." I plop down next to him and snuggle in. He throws his arm around me.

"If you start your own business, you probably won't have to take late calls."

I laugh at that. "Are you kidding me? I'll be working twenty-four seven when I start my own business."

"Tell me what you want." He lightly touches my hair, curls a strand around his finger. "What do you envision this business of yours to be like?"

"I want a pet store, and I...well, it's silly now."

"What's silly now?"

I look at him, and see the genuine curiosity in his eyes. "When I was little, I always wanted to be a vet, but then Gavin… and don't get me wrong, I don't regret Gavin. He's the best thing that has ever happened to me. But I guess life happened, circumstances changed, and that dream is a thing of the past."

"No way, Harper." The conviction in his voice catches me off guard. "You can still make that happen."

I shrug. "Maybe someday I'll be a vet, with my own practice and my own pet store. Right after I win the lottery," I tease. "Was being a professional hockey player always your dream?"

"Yeah."

"Have you given any thought to what you'll do when you finish playing?"

"I thought about becoming a dog walker, but it turns out I'm not very good at it."

I laugh and whack his stomach. "Come again with me tomorrow. You can only get better."

"Hey, play nice."

"What?" I say, feigning innocence and loving our easy banter. "That was a compliment."

"It was an insult wrapped up to sound like you had faith in me."

"I do have faith in you, big daddy."

As soon as those words leave my mouth, heat dances in his eyes. He picks up the remote, shuts the TV off, and pulls me to my feet. "You want big daddy, you're going to get big daddy." I yelp as he scoops me up and I'm sure I've never seen him take his stairs so fast. I simply love the way this man reacts to me, the way he looks at me and wants me.

He carries me to the bed and sets me on it. Two seconds later he's standing before me, naked, and I crook my finger, beckoning him close.

"Can't forget this," he says and pulls a condom from the nightstand. "Don't want to tempt fate twice, right?"

Something in the way he posed that question makes me think he's asking if I *do* want to tempt fate twice, but I must be mistaken. He told me straight up he didn't want kids. Is it possible that's changed over the last month?

He climbs over me, and presses his lips to mine, and the next thing I know, I'm naked and he's moving inside me. We hold each other tight, and as my heart pounds hard in my chest and my emotions take a rollercoaster ride, I make the decision to talk to him. First thing tomorrow, I'm going to open up, tell him I don't want this hook-up to end. Although I'm not sure he's up for a ready-made family, a big brother and big daddy is one thing, but taking on a family full time is something else entirely.

I push that from my thoughts, and concentrate on the pleasure building inside me, and before I know it, we both climax, and my eyes slip shut as we hold one another. He pulls out of me, cleans us up and pulls me against his warm body. His soft sounds fill the room as he sleeps and my eyes creep open as thoughts once again invade, beat against my brain, and I stare at the ceiling for a very long time before I finally succumb to sleep. When I wake, I reach across the bed, only to find it empty. I jackknife up and check the time. I stifle a yawn and throw my feet over the bed as I call out to Liam, but the house is silent.

I pull on the sweats I wore last night, and a T-shirt and head downstairs. I search the counter for a note, but find none. I snatch my phone from the counter, and read a text from Liam, letting me know he had to run out and I was sleeping so soundly he didn't want to wake me. A small smile pulls at me and I guess we'll have to wait until later to have that talk.

I make a pot of coffee, and wander through his house drinking it. Someone raps on the door, and my heart jumps, only to realize it's not Liam coming home because he wouldn't knock on his own damn door. I hurry across the room and pull open the door, and the second I see who's on the steps, I nearly drop my coffee mug. I falter back a bit, my brain rushing to catch up.

"What...what do you want?"

"Now, is that any way to greet me?" Devon says, and opens his arms wide like he expects me to jump into them as he tries to look past my shoulders.

I square my shoulders and put on my best kick-ass face, not that I have a kick-ass face, but no way am I going to let him think he's intimidating me, even though he is. "You need to go."

His smirk raises the hair on the back of my neck. "Can't an old friend come by and say hello?"

"We are not friends, and if you don't leave, I'll call the police."

"Aww, come on, Harper." He angles his head and a sick feeling swirls in my stomach as his gaze drops to take me in like I'm a juicy steak. "Don't be like that." I go to shut the door, and he puts his foot out to stop it. "Just wanted to come by and see the nice set-up you have."

My heart beats a little faster, and I shake my head. How did I not see what a creep this guy really was? How did I let him into my life—Gavin's life—and think he was one of the good guys? God, I am such a bad judge of character.

"Where's your sugar daddy?" he asks.

"He's not my sugar daddy."

"Maybe not, and maybe he's not who you think he is."

I stare at him, hating the doubt he's putting in my head, that he could so quickly make me doubt Liam. I've admitted numerous times that I was a bad judge of character, but I'm not wrong about Liam. He is one of the good ones. I'm sure of it.

"We're friends," I shoot back.

His smirk widens. "Is that why you're wearing his clothes?"

"What do you want?" I glare at him, and hate the way my hand is shaking as I hold my coffee cup. "You took everything I had, Devon. I have nothing left to give."

"We'll see," he says and pulls his foot back. I slam the door shut, and nearly collapse against it. Goddammit! He clearly saw the picture, and here he is, just like I expected, sniffing around looking for...something. I wish I could have seen through his façade before I let him into my life, before he charmed his way into my bank account. At least with Liam, I know it's not my money he's after. I don't have any. He's not using me for anything, and I never should have dragged him into my life. Maybe I should just pick up my son and stay as far away from Liam as possible. He doesn't need my troubles.

I pinch my eyes shut and shake my head because running away means loss for Gavin, and I swore when I got involved with Liam, I wouldn't do anything to jeopardize his relationship with my son. Now I'm left with two choices. Run and forget this ever happened, severing what I think is blossoming and risk ruining things between Liam and Gavin—which will protect Liam, but hurt Gavin. Or stay and take a chance that what's between us is the real deal, which could either be the best thing ever.

What the hell am I going to do?

For the last week, I've been crazy busy, running around town with my buddy Cole, and making real estate appointments. Harper seemed a bit suspicious about my sudden absence, leaving the house early, coming in late, but the truth is, she's been acting a bit strange herself, and I'm not sure why. When I came home that morning after leaving her in bed, she seemed upset, perturbed by something, but she brushed it off as work. I wasn't so sure, but she didn't seem like she wanted me to press, so I let it go.

Maybe it was nothing more than her trying to hide my birthday 'surprise party' at Nina's house. Afterward, I plan to open up to Harper and show her exactly what I've been up to. I just hope I'm not reading things wrong here, and she wants what I want. I can't leave here next week without laying it all on the line and proving to her that we'd have an amazing future together.

"So, we're just getting out for a drive, huh? You wanted to see the Great Wheel?" I ask, knowing full well she's driving around town to throw me off and that we'll be headed to Cole's any second now.

"Yeah, it's just been a long time," she says as she maneuvers her car through the streets, insisting on driving, even though any second now I'm worried about the muffler or something a little more important falling off the vehicle. "You've been so distracted lately, I thought it would be nice to do something fun."

I can almost hear the question in that statement, asking me why I've been so distracted, but I can't tell her. That would ruin the surprise.

"You've been a bit distracted yourself."

"Work," she says so quickly, her usual answer, and I try not to dwell on it or let the past invade my brain and send me down the rabbit hole. She's nothing like the women who hang out at the rink, and is not looking for anything from me.

"How come you got a sitter for Gavin? I'm sure he'd love the wheel too," I push.

"Oh, he wanted to see Holden, and he doesn't like heights, so I thought it was best to leave him with Violet for the night. He's fine."

"He's staying the whole night, then?"

"Yeah. You sure are full of questions tonight," she says and bites her lip. Is she trying really hard not to spill the beans? From everything I've learned about her, she's not the kind of girl who is good at keeping secrets.

"I have one more."

Her eyes hold a measure of worry, and I soothe it when I ask, "Do you always wear a sexy black dress when you're exploring downtown Seattle?"

"You think it's sexy?"

I laugh hard at that, because that's exactly the kind of evasive answer I'd give. "Yeah, I find it sexy. But you turn me on in your little summery dresses full of dog hair, remember."

Her soft chuckles warm me from the inside out. "A warm breeze turns you on, Liam."

"Hey," I say, feigning insult. "I resemble that comment." What can I say, I'm a red-blooded male, but truth be told, neither a warm breeze or puck bunny does it for me anymore. Harper is the only woman who turns me on. Things have changed drastically for me since hooking up with her. I reach up and grab the 'oh shit' bar and she turns to me, her lips tight, her eyes narrowing in on me.

"Hey, I know how to drive."

I arch a brow when a clanking sound rattles beneath the car, and I look over to see her check engine light on. I make a mental note to get her car checked out for her, or better yet, buy her a new one, although she's not the kind of girl who accepts gifts, and honestly, I do love that about her. It's a refreshing break.

"It's not your driving I'm worried about," I inform her.

She whacks my stomach and I take her hand, bring it to my mouth and kiss it.

"Sweet little Dixey here has not let me down yet."

"You call your car Dixey?" I take in the tiny smile on her face and sense a story. "Spill," I say.

She laughs. "You sound like Violet and Emma. They were all over me to tell secrets at Jason's birthday party."

"Did you?"

"Honestly, I didn't have to. One look at us and they knew. But I sort of said I was tapping you."

I laugh out loud. "My God, the things that come out of that sweet mouth of yours."

"Maybe it's not so sweet."

"It's sweet. You're sweet."

I'm fucking in love with you.

She takes her eyes off the street for a second to turn my way and honest to God, as cliché as it might sound, she really does take my breath away. Tonight, her blonde hair is up, perfectly styled, and the strands that are falling around her face are on purpose, not because the clip can't contain them. A hint of blush sculptures her cheekbones, and brings out the blue in her eyes. There is no way on the face of this earth that I can leave here next week without knowing she'll be here for me when I return. I have one weekend left to convince her that we should be a family and add to it. She never did go get that morning after pill. She started her period right away, and as much as I hated to talk about a girl's period in the past—juvenile, I know—I like that she's open about her body with me. Heck, I even ran out to pick up her tampons. In the past, I might have thought something like that would force me to cash in my man card, but you know what? That's bullshit. It makes me more of a man to help her like that. It makes me a better man. She makes me a better man by allowing me to be who I really am all the time, not just behind closed doors.

I think about a future with her, and how she talked about ending things when the picture of us came out. I can handle anything her ex wants to throw at me, and I'm relieved that nothing came from the photo. Well, I guess what I should say is I'm glad nothing negative came from it. My coach loved it and so did the media. Lots of great publicity, and no sign of her ex. I'm pretty sure he wouldn't dare show his face when I'm around. I definitely would have left my mark on him, fuck the coach and fuck the contracts. Harper and her son come first. But I don't want to think about that right now. No, we don't have a lot of time left before I leave and I damn well want to make the most of every minute.

"I had this mare growing up. She was ancient. Every year my father said she'd never make it through the winter, but every spring she came out kicking." I love the smile on her face as she takes a happy trip down memory lane. After getting to know her, it's clear she doesn't have too many good memories, but the future is a different beast and I plan to make hers and Gavin's amazing, if she'll let me. "She was so feisty."

"And her name was Dixey."

"Look at you," she teases with a grin. "Hot and smart."

"You think I'm hot?" I reach across the seat and put my hand on her bare thigh. Her little intake of breath washes over me and strokes my thickening cock. I slide my hand up, and the heat from her sex warms the blood rushing through my veins. "How about we skip the wheel and go somewhere private?" She casts me a fast glance and I love the flush on her face. Love that she wants the same thing I do. In the bedroom, for now, and hopefully out of the bedroom before the end of the weekend.

"While that sounds fabulous, Liam, I really had my heart set on taking a ride on the wheel."

"I promise I can give you something better to ride on."

A laugh bubbles out of her throat, and I fucking love the ease of being with her. My heart squeezes tight in my chest. Jesus, I have never loved anyone the way I love her. "Maybe later," she says.

"Promise."

Her smile is sweet and demure. "I promise."

She takes a right instead of a left, and I give her thigh a squeeze. "You're going the wrong way."

"Right, I just remembered Gavin left his favorite video game at Nina and Cole's. Since we're close, do you mind if we stop in and grab it?"

My God, she is so bad at this, but I truly love her more for trying. "Don't mind at all." I sit back and keep the grin from my face.

"Do they know we're coming?"

"Ah no. You don't think they'll mind if we just pop by, do you?"

I reach for my phone. "I can text Cole. Let him know we're close."

She nods. "Oh, that's a great idea."

I fire off a text to Cole, and tap my fingers against the dashboard, and sing along—albeit horribly, but at least Harper seems entertained—to the music. She drives to Cole's place, and the lights are off and there are no cars in the driveway.

Either they aren't home or they're going all out to surprise me.

"Did you hear back from him?" Harper asks, like she's worried he's not home.

I glance at my phone. "It says they had to go out, but they left the game on the patio table out back, under the pergola."

"Good thing you texted and caught them just before they left."

I nod as she pulls into the driveway and kills the ignition. I feel like a prick. Deep inside, I love my teammates, my friends, but this kind of big party is so not what I want. Sure, in the past I could drink and pull it off, but I don't want that now. I want to snuggle up somewhere quiet with Harper. But if Nina and everyone wants to have a party for me, I'm going to be grateful and honestly, it doesn't seem so bad with Harper at my side.

"Why don't you wait here?" I say, just playing with her. "I'll run out back and grab the game, and then we get straight to the wheel."

"Oh, okay," she says and frowns and I feel a tinge of guilt for making her think hard about this.

"Actually, you'd better come. There's probably a lot of toys laying around and I don't want to grab the wrong thing."

Her face lights up and she jumps from the car, and I meet her at the hood. I slide my hand into hers, and glance around the quiet neighborhood. Of course, we're in a high-class area, and the houses are spread apart here, just like they are where I live. I have to say, though, I don't mind the area where Harper lives either and if that's where she wants to make home when we...

Okay, dude, don't get ahead of yourself.

She smiles up at me and glances around, her brow furrowed. Is she wondering where all the cars are and that maybe she messed up the date? With the sun low on the horizon, we follow the path to the backyard, and just as I suspected, when we get there, everyone jumps out and screams surprise. I put my hand on my chest. No way am I ruining this for Harper. I pretend they all scared the shit out of me.

I turn to find Harper grinning from ear to ear. "Surprise," she says. Unable to help myself, I lean down and press my lips to hers.

"You were behind this?"

"Not really," she says, her lashes blinking as she glances around, dictating that she just might know how much I hate this. "Were you surprised?"

"Very," I tell her. I make a point of not lying but I'm not going to burst her balloon here. I kiss her again, and someone screams "Get a room!" and I whisper in her ear, "Not a bad idea."

She chuckles. "First, you enjoy your party." I lift my head and glance around, but her hand on my arm has me turning back to her. "Liam."

"Yeah?"

"Are you okay with this?"

My heart squeezes so tight it's almost impossible to draw in air. Seeing her concern, knowing she understands more about me than I ever thought she would, I nod. "As long as you're here with me, I'm fine."

"Okay, let's go get you a drink."

"How about you drink, I'll drive."

"Nope, it's your birthday." She goes up on her toes, and despite the audience, puts her arms around me, and says, "You've been taking care of me, and now it's my turn to take care of you." She kisses me and everyone chuckles as she goes back on her heels.

"Sounds like you have something planned for later." She blinks and begins to whistle as she looks around innocently. "Come on," I say, my heart light and happy. Hand in hand, and with her by my side, we mingle with our friends, and when a beer is thrust into my hand, I accept, and spend the rest of my time nursing it. I'm not sure what she has planned, but I want to stay sober so I can savor every second of it.

Harper eventually excuses herself as the women break off and begin chatting. Every few seconds, I glance at her, and my heart soars as she laughs and shares stories with my friends— her friends now too.

The guys and I all hang out over the food table, snacking on sandwiches and potato chips. We mostly talk about hockey and the upcoming season. As the guys talk, Cole puts his hand on my shoulder and in a low voice says, "I know you don't love these things, but Nina was itching to get the gang together before we take off, and your birthday was the perfect excuse." I glance at my buddy, and it's clear he too can see who I really am.

"It's fine. You should have seen Harper trying to keep it a secret," I say and that's when I notice the smirk on Cole's face. I glance around to find all the guys smirking at me. "What?" They continue to grin. "Fine. I like her."

"No shit," Alek says. "You can't stop looking at her and thinking about her."

My gaze flies to Harper's again, and she's smiling at me. "I'm fucked, aren't I?" I say and the guys all start to laugh.

"Never thought I'd see the day," Cason says. "But it looks good on you, buddy."

Just then the team's newest rookie comes around the corner. Jesus, were we all that fresh faced once? Rider waves him over, and Cole hands him a beer. He's a little shy, like most of us were when we were first recruited. It's not easy walking into a room full of professional players.

"Sorry I'm late," he says, glancing around like he was worried this was some hazing party for him, but we're not assholes like some of the guys on the other teams. "Stuck in traffic." He takes a big swig of beer. "So, this is really a birthday party for Liam?"

Cole laughs. "Relax, Wes, enjoy yourself."

Just then Jules calls Rider over, and for a minute I'm worried she's going into labor, but no, it appears she just wants to tell him something. As she talks with her hands, very animated, everyone breaks off and the group begins to mingle as one again. I watch her for a second and the sudden image of a pregnant Harper, carrying my child, floods my brain and it's not a scary image at all.

With a smile on my face, I excuse myself to make a quick trip to the boys' room. I glance at Harper, but she's too distracted, punching something into her phone to even know I'm headed inside. Who the hell is she texting? I shake all worry from my brain. She's a single mother for Christ's sake. Of course, she's just checking in on Gavin. By the time I come back, the rookie is chatting up my girl.

My girl?

Damn right she's my girl. Needing to lay claim, show possession in some ridiculous caveman style, I walk up to them, and slide my arm around Harper's waist, pulling her against me. Her body is soft, warm and pliable as I hold her to me, her soft curves meshed against my hardness as she puts her hand on my chest, right about the vicinity of my pounding heart. Wes just gives me a grin—yeah, I know I'm being an asshole, and maybe someday he'll understand. I chuckle at that, because I was once like Wes, grinning as my friends all fell in love and thinking it would never happen to me. I guess there's someone for everyone, and you need to open your damn eyes to see that. Wes takes a small step back, putting distance between himself and the girl who is mine. Good call, buddy.

"Wes was just telling me he grew up in Canada," Harper says.

If he keeps looking at Harper the way he is, I'm going to buy him a one-way ticket back. "Yeah, Nova Scotia. I know."

"I've always wanted to visit Nova Scotia," Harper says. "It sounds so pretty."

"My family has a farm there. A big old farmhouse with lots of rooms. You're always welcome to visit."

A growl I have no control over rumbles in my throat and Harper turns to me. "You okay?"

"Yeah, I think it's time we get out of here."

She arches a brow. "Are you ready for your birthday surprise?"

"I don't need any more surprises tonight, Harper." I put my hand around her neck and pull her mouth to mine. I drop a possessive kiss onto her mouth, and from my periphery, I spot Wes walking away. I break the kiss and we're both breathless. "I only need you."

"I think you can have both."

Tell her, Liam. Tell her you want it all...

HARPER

My little car chugs along, holding its own as I drive through Mount Rainer National Park. My insides are full of love and happiness as I take a quick glance at my rugged hockey player, and find him grinning at me.

"Are we going for a hike?" he asks. He hasn't shut up since we left the party, quizzing me on where I'm taking him.

"It's dark, and there are wild animals in this park. Do you think that's my jam, Liam?" I ask.

He laughs out loud. "I wouldn't put anything by you. You're full of surprises, and I love that about you."

Love?

Did he just use the word love? My heart beats a little faster as I stare straight ahead, carefully negotiating the road. I chew on that for a moment, toss it around in my brain and I'm about to overthink it when Liam's hand lands on my lap.

"Look."

He points up ahead, and in my lights, I catch a flash of white as a deer crosses the road. "So pretty," I say. "I once saw a black bear in the park. Gavin and I came here, camping with Violet, Jason, and Holden. It was a few years ago."

"Ah, so we're going camping then."

"I only sleep on the ground when I have to. I prefer a cozy bed, thank you very much."

He leans toward me, and I swear I'm about to pull over and jump on his lap right here when his scent curls around me, tickles between my legs. "I don't care where I sleep. As long as you're beside me."

"You didn't mind my small bed?"

"Didn't even notice." My body tingles all over, loving the warmth in his voice, the softness, and the way he didn't mind hanging out at my small house, when his is so much more elaborate. He might be financially stable now, but he grew up in a middle-class family and seems very grounded. I really love that about him. There is that 'L' word again. But I'm far past denying that's what I feel for him.

I pick up my phone, and check the directions, and he falls silent beside me, staring out the window. He breaks the quiet and says, "I've never been chauffeured around before."

"I'm sure you have."

"Okay, well a time or two, but never by a beautiful woman who I can't wait to get my mouth on."

I chuckle and when the cabins come into view, I slow my vehicle and take the road to the main lobby. Liam sits up a bit straighter. "What are you up to, Harper?"

I put my car into park, kill the ignition and turn to him. "I thought a private birthday party for two was more your style."

He nods and smiles at me. "You're right about that." I'm about to head inside the lodge to get our keys when his frown stops me.

"What?"

"This place..." He closes his mouth and frowns like he's not sure how to put it.

Panic surges inside me. Shit, did I make a mistake. It's not a huge, fancy-ass hotel in town, but I know this man, and he's not about that at all. "You don't like it."

"I love it, Harper. It's pretty much the nicest thing anyone has ever done for me, but..."

I stare at him and that's when understanding hits like a puck to the face. "It's covered," I say. "I've been saving."

"I thought you were saving for your own business."

"I am, and if it has to wait a little longer, so be it." I lean into him and put my lips on his. His hand automatically slides around my neck, and he holds me to him as he kisses me softly. We break apart, and I glance around. "Instead of giving the animals a show, how about we go check out our cabin."

He stares at me in the dark car, the light coming from the lodge spilling over us. His gaze moves over my face and my body warms all over at the way this man looks at me. "I'll just be a sec, okay?"

"I can—"

I put my fingers to his lips. "This is your birthday party. Tonight, it's all about you."

"As long as I can put my mouth on you, I'm happy."

Smiling at that, I grab my purse and leave him in the car as I duck inside the main lodge, which is a great big beautiful log cabin, a fire burning in the gigantic hearth. I quickly sign us in and get our room keys. A few minutes later, I pull up to our secluded log cabin, and park in the driveway.

"What a view," Liam says.

I glance around. "Gorgeous."

"Yeah, gorgeous."

I turn back and find him looking at me, and fall just a little more for him, which is a huge surprise, because I'm not even sure that's possible. "Let's go check it out."

We exit my car, and I walk to the truck, where I pull out a bag containing clothes and things for both of us.

"I guess you had this all planned out, didn't you?" We take the two small steps to the door, and I slide in the key. The door opens to showcase a rustic yet cozy cabin with a fireplace, kitchen, bathroom and bedroom, and a gorgeous view of the mountain. On the table sits a birthday cake in the shape of a hockey stick, and balloons are tied to the chair. He turns to me.

"Is this what all those secret phone calls were about?"

I shrug one shoulder. "Maybe."

"Get over here." He pulls me to him, and my body meshes against his as he gives me a very passionate kiss that tells me just how much he likes his surprise. He breaks the kiss and pushes my hair from my shoulders. "I can't believe you arranged all this. It must have been a lot of trouble."

"No trouble at all. Just a few, or many, phone calls." I chuckle. "How about a slice of cake?"

"Sounds good, as long as I can follow it with a taste of you."

"Come on, let's light the candle and you..." I tap him on the nose. "can make a birthday wish." We step up to the cake, and I fish a lighter from my purse.

He laughs. "You really thought of everything. Wait, how come there's only one candle?"

"Because this is a log cabin, and we don't want to burn it down. You're not a teenager anymore, Liam."

He laughs. "I'm only thirty, and you're not too far behind."

I light the candle, stand behind him and wrap my arms around his waist. "Don't forget to make a wish when you blow it out." I hold him tight, and put my head on his strong back, closing my eyes and making my own wish and hoping his is the same. His back expands as he takes in a big breath and lets it out in a puff.

I let him go, and he throws his arm around me. "What did you wish for?" I ask.

"Come on, you know as well as I do that I can't tell you. It won't come true if I do."

"You're right, don't tell me." I step away and find two plates and a knife. "I want all your wishes to come true." I set the plates on the table, and glance at Liam. His head is angled, and his eyes are a darker shade of brown as he looks at me.

"You really do, don't you?"

"Of course, I do."

He shakes his head. "I've never met a woman quite like you." I open my mouth, but he holds his hand up to stop me. "That's a good thing."

"You know what else is a good thing?"

"What?"

"This double chocolate cake. I've been salivating since ordering it last week."

He takes the knife from me. "Then let's not keep you waiting another second." He cuts a generous piece, and I grab the champagne from my bag.

I hold it up. "How about some bubbly on the deck? The view is too good not to enjoy."

"It might be a bit cold."

"I'm a single mom, Liam. I'm tough."

He laughs. "Yeah, you're tough. I won't even deny that."

"But I'd still like for you to open this bottle."

He chuckles as I hand it over, and he pops it open. A few minutes later, with our plates of cake and champagne, we head out onto the back deck which has a glass railing, so nothing hampers the view. The cooler night air wisps over our skin in the breeze and a sense of contentment curls around me. When was the last time I felt so safe, and so happy. We sit in the Adirondack chairs, and I exhale as peace fills my soul.

"I hope I'm the reason for that smile on your face, and not that big-ass piece of cake."

I laugh at that. "Would you be upset if I said both?"

"Nah, I could never be mad at you." He cuts into a big chunk of cake and slides it into his mouth. "Jesus," he says, the word coming out mumbled. "This is amazing. I mean, it's not your lava cake, nothing can compare to that, but it's delicious."

"I couldn't make a lava cake and get it here without you knowing. But I know this baker, her shop is right beside the pet store, and this is her creation, made just for you."

I take a big bite, and my eyes roll back into my head as a moan crawls out of my throat. "This is almost as good as sex," I tease.

"Hey..."

"Almost," I say as an idea forms. "I just had an idea for the best mind-blowing orgasm."

He perks up, his shoulders squaring as he sits a little straighter. "I'm listening."

I laugh, and it feels light and airy. "I thought you would be." I set my cake on the table beside me, stand, and glance around to ensure we're alone and that no one can see us from our deck. The cabins are spaced apart, and only the forest creatures can see the show, so I reach behind my back to unzip my dress. I shimmy, and Liam's chest expands with his deep intake of breath as the fabric falls to my feet.

"You are so beautiful," he says as light from inside spills out and falls over my nakedness. He makes a move to stand, but I shake my head. His brow arches as he stays put, and I'm not sure why, but I feel like putting on a show for him. I wiggle my hips, and a smile tugs at his lips.

"What are you doing, Harper?"

"Trying something new to make things interesting?"

He adjusts his pants, and I'd imagine he's very uncomfortable sitting there with an erection. "I'm already interested."

God, I love his enthusiasm. I reach behind my back, unhook my bra and slide it off my arms. As my breasts spill free, his groan of encouragement tingles along my spine. He scrubs his face, and a soft curse reaches my ears when I dip my finger into the icing, and put a dab on my nipple.

"Fuck me hard," he says and I laugh. I get it, this is out of character for me, something he surely doesn't expect, but I want to tease him, want to open up and have fun. I grin at him. "Not funny, Harper."

"You're not having fun."

"You know that's not what I mean, and you don't have to do this, not for me."

"Are you saying you don't like it?"

"Fuck no, I'm not saying that. I love everything you do."

"Then why don't you sit there like a good big daddy, and let me take care of you."

I swirl my finger in the icing again, put a dollop on my other nipple, and slide my finger into my mouth. I suck hard, mimicking what I want to do to him, and he pushes to his feet. This time, I don't stop him. Not that I think I could. Nope, I'd have more luck holding the Shooters' entire defensive team back than stopping him.

He closes the distance in three long strides, and his hands span my waist. "You're fucking killing me."

"Not my intention."

"Want to know mine?" he asks.

"Sure," I say but I already know them, judging by the heat in his eyes. He bends and takes my nipple into his mouth and his growl of want echoes in the forest around us. I grab fistfuls of his hair as he eats at me, going from one breast to the other, like he can't decide which tastes better. "Sex and chocolate. Who fucking knew it could be this good?" His hands slide down my body, and he dips into my panties. Another growl cuts through the dark night when he finds me sopping wet. He tears his mouth from my nipple, dragging rough teeth over it as he does. "I need you naked."

"First this," I say, and pop the button on his pants. I drag them down his legs, and take his boxer shorts with me. He kicks them off and takes my shoulders, and while I can't wait to have him inside me, I need to taste him first. I dip into the icing and drag my finger over his rock-hard cock, and he pulses beneath my touch.

I take him into my mouth, and the flavor of his skin, combined with the chocolate, is like a party on my tongue. His hips move, and he slides into my throat, his hands moving my hair from my face to watch. I lick him clean, and drink in his pre-cum as his growls echo in the night. While I'd like to stay on my knees all night, he has other plans. He grips my shoulders and pulls me to my feet. His hands go around my body, and he grips my ass, and tugs until I'm wrapped around his hips.

He clears the table with a smooth sweep, my cake and dish landing on the deck, and he grabs his shirt, putting it under me. My dress, all balled up, is used for a pillow and I like how my comfort is important to him.

"Stay just like that," he says and fishes a condom from his pocket. I made an appointment and went to the doctor to get on the pill, but it's too soon to go without another form of protection. Later though, down the road—if, like me, he wants to continue this relationship—we won't need one and I can't wait to feel skin on skin.

He sheaths himself, and takes my legs to put them around his back. With one hard push, he's inside me, moving, and stroking deep, his thumb on my clit, his eyes on mine. Time seems to stand still, as we stare at one another and he leans over me, pressing his pelvis to my body as he threads his fingers through mine, forging a physical connection...an emotional bond. My heart swells with everything I feel for this man, and no words need to be said, because I'm sure he's feeling everything just as much as I am.

"Liam," I whisper into the night, that one word letting him know everything.

"Harper," he whispers in return as he takes me higher and higher. My body breaks, and I clench around him. He curses slightly, and throws his head back as he finds his own release.

He falls over me, and as we hug one another tight, I'm sure in this moment that this is the real thing and nothing and no one can come between us. As soon as that pops into my head, old insecurities creep in but I push them down. I have to be right about us. The alternative could very well mean heartache for me...and my son.

LIAM

I glance at the gorgeous woman beside me as she maneuvers her car down the winding road. My heart pounds just a little faster when she turns my way and gifts me with a sweet smile. She places her hand over her mouth to cover her yawn, and yeah, I get it. I'm exhausted too. We spent the best part of the night making love, and you'd think this morning I'd be sated, but no. There is no way on earth that I'll ever get enough of this woman.

"You're staring," she says, and I put my hand on her thigh, needing the constant contact.

I still can't believe she set last night up for me, going through the trouble of balloons and cake, and it really was a big surprise. I guess she can keep secrets better than I thought she could.

"Your point?" She simply laughs at me, and I check the time on my phone.

Her brows lift. "Somewhere you need to be?"

"Actually, yeah," I say. She's not the only one who can keep a secret when need be. She looks back at the road and the love I have for her expands inside my chest. I take a deep fueling breath.

"I have a busy day too. I have to pick up Gavin and get to the store. Charlie will be in for his bath, and then this afternoon I have to walk a few dogs."

"A dog walker's work is never done." Usually I go with her, but this afternoon, I'm going to be all tied up. "I guess you'll be glad when you're running the business yourself and can make your own hours."

"That would be a dream come true."

I grin, wanting to make every dream she's ever had come true. "I'll meet you back at the house for dinner. We'll order in?"

"Sounds good," she says and for a quick second, I think I spot something in her eyes, something that looks like concern, but when I squeeze her leg, she gifts me with another big smile and I chalk that uneasy look up to exhaustion. I could use a good nap too, and kind of feel bad for keeping her up all night when she has work this morning.

We fall into a comfortable silence as she drives and I take in the scenery. A short while later, she drops me at my place. Before I get out of her car, I lean into her and place a soft kiss on her mouth.

"Thanks for last night," I whisper into her mouth. "That was the best birthday present ever."

Her smile is soft and warm, her eyes a bit dazed as she sits there with her mouth poised open, like she's waiting for more kisses, and dammit, I plan to give them to her. Now. Tomorrow. Forever. I glance at my phone again, and she straightens in her seat.

"I'd better get going."

"Yeah, you don't want to be late," she says, even though she has no idea what I'm up to.

I reluctantly open the door, not wanting to go, but knowing I have to. "Drive safely," I say, before using a great deal of force to close her door. The damn thing looks like it's ready to fall off the hinges. After my meeting, maybe I'll head to the car dealership and look around. Then again, I appreciate my nut sack and she's likely to neuter me if she came back here and found a new car, just for her. I chuckle at that. She's not the kind of girl to take gifts of such grandeur. If I was her fiancé, however...

I stand in the driveway as she backs out and disappears down the road. I hurry inside, do a quick change of clothes, and jump in my truck. Fifteen minutes later, I stop to pick up Cole, who's been helping me with my search.

"You took off early last night," he says with a grin. "Didn't even hang around for cake."

"I had cake," is all I say.

His grin widens. "Enjoy the mountains?"

I laugh. "Is there anything you don't know?"

"No, I know everything. The girls talk."

I back out of his driveway, and we talk about nothing as we drive to the downtown core. I squeeze my big truck into a tight spot and slam it into park. Harper isn't going to like me going behind her back like this, but I'm doing it anyway. I don't want to just tell her how I feel about her, I want to show her in a big way.

Cole and I jump from the truck and the realtor is standing outside a shopping complex, reading something on his phone when I reach him. "Hey Liam, Cole," he says and lifts his head.

I glance at the strip of stores along the street. While this is a great location, I'm not sure about parking, but decide to check the space out anyway. For the next three hours, the real estate agent takes Cole and me from one location to the next, and I'm exhausted by the time we're finished.

"Want to go grab a cold one?" Cole asks. "Sit down and do the pros and cons of each place?"

I check my phone. I don't think Harper will be finished just yet, so I nod. "Sounds like a great idea."

Back in my truck, we drive to Nelly's, which is pretty quiet this time of day. Cole gestures the server for a couple of beers and I fish my phone from my back pocket, checking to see if Harper has texted me. For the next little while, we lay out the pros and cons to each place we viewed, and we both come up with the same answer. The house just a few blocks from her home with backyard greenspace, room for expansion, and a park nearby. We could easily change the front to look more like a business, and she could convert the upper part of the house to an apartment and live in it if she wants, so Gavin would be able to go to school with Holden, and during the summers, my off-season, they could stay at my place—where there is always room for Holden and his other friends.

From my periphery, that guy Griff, who'd questioned me on Harper, comes through the front door. "Do you know that guy?" I ask Cole, an uneasy feeling mushrooming inside me when his eyes meet mine, and he gives a curt nod. I don't believe in coincidences and the fact that he's here again, four o'clock on a Saturday afternoon, raises all kinds of questions.

"No, why?" Cole asks.

The server comes with our drinks, and I take a big mouthful. "I don't know. He rubs me the wrong way."

Cole cracks his knuckles. "Want me to go rub him the wrong way?"

I snort. "Nah, I can fight my own battles."

Griff takes a seat, orders a beer, and gets on his phone. Every few seconds, he glances my way, and I'm about to go over there and ask him what his problem is when my phone pings. I glance down and notice it's Jeremy, but I'm not in the mood to talk to anyone at the moment—not while Griff is staring at me, like trouble is right around the corner. I flick off the volume, and turn it over, my eyes still on Griff.

"I think he's sweet on you," Cole says and sits up a little straighter, an intimidation pose that would put fear into any man. Griff downs his beer, stands, and tips his hat to me as he exits.

I take a long pull from the bottle, and set it on the counter harder than necessary. "What the fuck is that guy's problem?" Just then Rider and Kane come walking in, and we wave them over. For the next hour, we shoot the shit, and the place begins to fill up with suits and tech guys, getting off work.

I grab my phone to check the time and that's when I notice a dozen calls and texts from Jeremy.

Worry rakes through me, scraping along my skin. "Shit."

"What's wrong?" Rider asks.

"Don't know. Jeremy's been calling." I jump up worried that something happened to Harper or Gavin. "I have to call him."

I step away from the table and find a quiet corner. The second Jeremy answers, my stomach falls to the floor.

"Where are you? I've been trying to call for an hour."

"At Nelly's with the guys." I lift my head when a bunch of rowdy businessmen come in. I hold the phone tighter against my ear, and put my hand over the other. "What's up?"

"I'm at your place. Meet me here."

"Are Harper and Gavin okay?"

A pause and then. "Yeah, just get here, okay?"

"On my way." I end the call and hurry back to the table.

"What the hell, Liam?" Cole asks, his eyes narrowed with worry.

I rake a shaky hand through my hair. "Jeremy wants to see me." I glance at Cole, take in the stiffness in his body. "You want me to drop you—"

"No, I'll get a ride with one of the guys." He jerks his thumb toward Rider. "You'd better go see what he wants and keep me posted."

I nod, but then the bartender turns up the TV in the corner, and my gaze flies to it when I hear my name. "Mother fucker," I curse, and glance at the pictures of me right here in Nelly's with that girl that tried to climb me wrapped around my waist. "How the fuck—"

"Oh Christ," Cole says, and I grip the back of the chair and squeeze hard enough to break it.

"I guess we know what Jeremy wants," Kane says, as adrenaline floods my body. Has Harper seen this? Does she think I was out whoring with other women? Fuck, man, I need to talk to her and I need to talk to her now. "I gotta go."

Chairs scrape the floor as the guys stand, like they're ready to flee with me, but I'm out of there in seconds flat, and phone Harper from the truck. When it continues to ring and ring, I toss it aside, desperate to get to her. I start the car and grip the steering wheel hard enough to turn my knuckles white. I pull into traffic and drive like a goddamn madman as I hurry home, praying Harper is there.

I swallow to calm myself down. The fans are going to eat this up, and a woman wrapped around me wouldn't have been a big deal until Harper. I guess the media jumped on it, because I haven't been giving them anything to work with lately, and while I love my fans, I have to be who I really am. Being with Harper taught me that, and maybe I should only be caring for those who care about me. Let's face it, I give the fans what they want, but they don't know me, or care about me as a person.

But Harper is smart. She's not going to jump to the wrong conclusions, right? I mean, we're not officially together or anything, but she must know I'd never fuck around on her. I'm not like Gavin's father, or that douchebag ex of hers. What the hell was his name? Devon? I guess it doesn't matter. I just have to hope she believes enough in me to know I'd never do anything to hurt her, just like I know she'd never do anything to hurt me.

I finally make it home, and practically leap from the truck when I find Jeremy standing on my steps, the front door cracked open.

"Where's Harper?"

"Gone," he says and folds his arms across his barrel chest.

"Gone where?" I'm about to push past him and search the house for her things when he stops me. "I need to find her."

"She saw the photo of you with that girl, Liam. She was heading out, she looked kind of panicked, like she needed to get out of here, when I showed up. She had a big duffle bag in her hand, like she was fleeing. She stopped long enough to ask if I saw the pictures. I told her I did. She asked if I thought they were true, that you were with that girl."

"What did you tell her?"

"What do you think I told her, Liam? I wasn't going to lie about your reputation." He smirks.

"Nothing fucking happened, and now thanks to you, she thinks something did."

He gives me a look that suggests I might be dense. "I wouldn't be too worried about her, Liam. She was using you all this time. Don't worry, though, I told her you were using her, too." He smirks. "I let her know being photographed with a single mom dog walker was all about your image."

"Why the fuck would you do that?" I fist my hands, and if I wasn't in too much of a hurry to straighten this out with Harper, I'd knock his fucking teeth out, but when it comes right down to it, he was going off my reputation—the Liam I presented to the world, not the Liam I really am. But Jesus, Jeremy was the one who set up the pictures of the two of us.

She doesn't know that, though. Now, she likely thinks I was behind them showing up at my door. "Wait, what do you mean she was using me too? Never mind. I don't have time for this. I have to go find her."

He grabs my arm and I shake him off. He arches a brow, like I shouldn't have done that and says, "You won't go searching for her when you hear what I'm about to tell you."

That stops me dead in my tracks. I square off against him. "What are you talking about?"

"All you saw was the pictures of the girl."

"Yeah, I was with the guys when they were splashed all over the that bullshit show, Dirt. But I wasn't joking, nothing happened. Someone set that up for the photos." My mind goes back to Griff and the way he was smirking at me. What the hell, though? Who am I to him? My mind comes to a screeching halt. Did Harper ever tell me Devon's last name? Is it possible it's Griff? Fuck me. "Griff had to be behind it," I murmur to myself.

"That woman just threw herself at me, and I think I know who was behind it."

"Do you know who's behind this?" He holds his phone out, and when the image of Harper and me having sex at the cottage last night plays out before me, my heart sinks into my gut, and my throat dries and crackles like tinder in a blazing fire.

"What the fuck?" My eyes meet Jeremy's. "Where did you get that?"

"The better question is, how did Dirt get a hold of it?"

I shake my head. "Dirt has this? All they showed was pictures of some random girl wrapped around me. I didn't see this."

Jeremy glares at me. "Maybe you should have hung around the bar a little longer, because they followed up with this."

Since my knees can no longer hold me, I sink down onto my stoop as Rider pulls into my driveway. The guys all spill out of the car, and slowly walk toward me. From the looks on their faces they saw the follow-up on Dirt.

"Hey," Cole says and sits down beside me. "That was from last night huh?"

"Yeah," I say my brain racing so fast, I don't know what to think.

"Who knew you were going to be there?" Jeremy asks.

I shrug. "I guess all the guys knew, and their wives, but none of them did this. I mean, it could have been anyone, right?" I won't believe Harper was responsible for this. I can't.

"I don't know what to say, bud. I think you need to talk to her."

I tug my phone from my pocket, and phone her. She doesn't answer, and my heart stalls when three little dots appear.

"She's texting," I say to no one in particular as my heart pounds in my ears.

I fill my lungs and hold my breath as those three dots appear for what feels like a lifetime. Jesus, is she writing a book? Her message finally comes in, and air leaves my lungs in a whoosh.

Thanks for all you've done with Gavin. He'll be in school soon, and you'll be on the road, so we'll be leaving the big brother program.

.   .   .

Formal. Curt. No mention of us, a future together—as a family—all the things I want. Nope, just a couple of words to effectively cut me out of their lives. "No fucking way," I say around the lump in my throat. "Why is she doing this?"

"Because she got what she wanted from you, Liam. She won the goddamn lottery with you," Jeremy points out. He huffs. "Why the hell do you look so shocked? This isn't the first time a girl screwed you over."

Won the lottery.

"She's not like that," I say, defending her through clenched teeth as old hurts surface. Harper knew who I really was. She saw and like the guy I was behind closed doors. I'm sure of it. She'd never sell me out...never.

He holds his phone up. "Who knew you were going to be in the mountains, outside on the deck having sex, for Christ's sake?"

I tug on my hair, and try to wrap my brain around all this bullshit. "I didn't even know I'd be having sex on the deck."

"Did Harper? Did she ask to go outside?" I resist the urge to punch Jeremy in the face just to shut him up, to stop putting doubts in my brain.

"Yes, but...it's not like that. She's not like that." I glance at my buddies. "Right? I mean you guys met her."

"I met her," Cole says. "I liked her a lot."

"You don't think she was behind this?"

"Liam—" he begins, a worried look on his face.

I shake my head and cut him off. "You're all fucking wrong."

Cole's brow furrows. "You two need to talk. That's all I was going to say. You love her. It's easy to see, and you wouldn't have fallen for her if deep inside you thought she could do something like this."

"She was running out of here when I arrived, Cole," Jeremy says, shaking his head at us like we're idiots. "All her things in a bag. Why do you think she was in such a hurry?"

I glare at him. "Because she saw the pictures and thought the worst." I exhale, and scrub my face. "I actually didn't think she'd react that way. I thought she'd at least want to hear my side." Then again, it doesn't sound like Jeremy was particularly nice to her, going straight for the jugular by telling her I was using her.

"She didn't hear you out because she was stabbing you in the back the whole time." I open my mouth, about to protest. "I'm guessing she got a fair bit of bucks for this," Jeremy says. "What did she need money for, Liam?" he asks.

I push to my feet. "I'm not listening to this shit anymore."

I jump in my truck, and Cole slides into the passenger side without a word. He stays silent, as I drive the streets—not aimlessly though, my subconscious has a destination in mind. Beside me, Cole checks his phone and shoots off a text, no doubt letting Nina know his whereabouts. I cast him a quick glance. I want what he has. I want it so fucking bad that I can taste it, and no way is anyone going to take that away from me.

"What the hell are we doing here?" Cole asks when I pull into Randy's Auto Repairs.

"Getting answers." I curl my fingers into fists. "With these."

"You're going to get yourself into trouble," Cole warns. "You know what this could mean for your career and sponsors, right?"

"Yup, but Harper is worth it."

He grins at me. "Let's do this then."

●18

HARPER

The only good thing about washing Charlie down is that he shakes every few minutes and soaks my clothes, face and hair. Why is that good, you ask? Oh, just because it hides the tears free-falling down my cheeks. It's been a couple of days since I found out the truth about Liam. Here I thought there was another side to the rule breaker. Thought he was just a soft and sensitive guy with a big heart, a guy who hid that side of himself and put on a show for the outside world—his fans. Was I really so wrong about him? Or when his sister said I was perfect for him, did it have more to do with cleaning up his image than the two of us really belonging together?

Ugh. I am so confused. My mind goes back to when Gavin and I had just gotten home, and I was carrying his duffle bag in from his sleepover, when I received a text from Violet, showing me the pictures of Liam with some girl wrapped around his waist. My first instinct wasn't to run away. No, it was to get to the bottom of the matter. I mean, I've seen pictures of Liam with lots of women in the past, and I came to all kinds of conclusions about him, only to discover, after spending so much time with him, that you can't judge a book by the cover.

You were wrong about him, Harper.

As that inner voice, one born from past hurts, pounds at me, my brain races, a part of me refusing to believe he's a cheater or a liar. Refusing to believe Jeremy who showed up at the door right behind me, even though he shoved the proof in my face, then followed it with the video of us, which totally confused me. Why would anyone want to video us? There was nothing about Liam to suggest he was fooling around behind my back. Sure, he was disappearing for hours on end, and I had no idea where he was going, and he wasn't offering up the information, but I trusted him.

You trusted before and look how that turned out.

But Liam's not Gavin's father, and he's not Devon. I take a fast breath and finish hosing down Charlie as Gavin plays with his toy cars beside me. I had to bring him to work with me today. Both Violet and Emma were busy, and his sitter Tera was packing for college. A humorless laugh catches in my throat. I hadn't needed anyone's help in a long time, because Liam was always there to take Gavin for me.

My God, what have I done? If I hadn't gotten involved with him, there'd be no embarrassing video of us, no reason for me to hang my head in shame, and Gavin would still have a big brother because I wouldn't be afraid to face Liam every day, knowing he was just using me.

Honestly, I'm still not sure how someone captured us on video. Was someone from the media following my car to the mountains, stalking us? Or was Devon somehow involved? Unease creeps through my veins, because if he could make a buck off it, I wouldn't put it past him. Maybe I should have told Liam that Devon showed up at his door, but the point is moot now. It's over between us, and I'm responsible for hurting my son.

A group of teens walk past us, pointing and snickering, and my throat squeezes tight, my face warm with humiliation. More and more customers are coming into the store, but it's not for their pets. No, it's to see me. The online magazine Dirt might have blanked out all of our private parts when they aired the video, but they didn't blank out my name, or what I did for a living. If Liam was using me, a struggling single mother and dog walker, to better his image, well, I guess that blew up in his face with the video.

"Mommy, are you crying?" Gavin asks.

I sniff and wipe my face. "No honey, Charlie just got me all wet."

He runs his car over the floor. "I miss my Liam."

The lump in my throat expands. "I know, Gavin. We can get you another big brother."

He lifts his car up and slams it on the floor. "I don't want another big brother. I want Liam."

Me too, kiddo. Me too.

"I want to play with Brandon and Casey!" he loudly whines, and guilt moves through me. I wasn't supposed to do anything to mess this up for my son, and I went ahead and did just that. He's losing Brandon and Casey and all his new friends because of this mess.

"Harper, can I speak to you?" I glance up to find Jon Welsh, my boss, and the owner of the pet store, standing over me, and my heart sinks into my stomach when I take in the frown on his face.

"Sure, just let me finish with Charlie here."

"That's okay." He snaps his fingers and Eric, almost sullenly, walks over. "Eric will finish up for you."

Eric gives me an apologetic smile, and that's when it occurs to me—I'm getting fired.

"Jon—" I begin, but he cuts me off.

"In my office please." I reach for Gavin's hand. "Why don't you let Eric look after him for a moment."

"I don't mind," Eric says. "Gavin, why don't you show me all your cars."

As Gavin gets out the rest of his toys, I follow Jon to his office. He takes a seat at his desk and I slowly sink into the chair across from him, my throat so tight I'm not sure I'll be able to speak.

"I'll get right to the point."

"I'm sorry," I push out. "I didn't mean for any of this to happen. I'm sure everything will die down soon, and everything will go back to normal."

"We can't take this bad publicity, and as much as I hate to, I'm going to have to let you go."

I open my mouth, but what's the point? He's not going to change his mind and no amount of begging from me is going to help. I'm a damn dog walker, a pet groomer, and I'll be replaced by the time I make it to the sidewalk. I snort. Liam replaced me before I even hit the sidewalk.

As that thought tumbles around inside my brain, my heart tightens. Nothing about Liam's actions, his deceit, feels right. But Jeremy assured me the pictures were real and I was nothing but a prop to help him clean up his image.

Were you though, Harper?

As I leave the office, and watch Gavin and Eric play, the last month flashes before my eyes. The Liam I got to know was nothing like the media portrayed. He was kind and caring, quiet and reflective. He seemed genuinely crushed and violated—betrayed—when he talked about the first sex video that was leaked. I get that I ran away without talking to him. Jeremy practically shoved me from the stoop. But if Liam wasn't with another woman like Jeremy said, wouldn't he have tried to talk to me? I mean, he did call, and I did say goodbye over text, but if what we had was real between us, and he was as upset by the pictures as I was—the video, even—wouldn't he have fought for me?

You're not fighting for him.

It's true, I'm not, and why is that? Am I afraid that he really is going to hurt me, that what we had wasn't real and was all in my head? That maybe I'm just not loveable? Have I made a huge mistake? Oh, God, I think I have. I need to talk to him, hear his side. I'm about to grab Gavin and run when fear invades once again.

Why isn't he trying to tell you his side, Harper?

I mull that over for a second, and as understanding dawns, my legs go weak and I nearly sink to the floor.

He thinks I'm behind the video!

Oh, God, I really need to talk to him. But would he even listen to me now? Would he even want to hear me, or believe in me? Lord knows, I jumped to the worst conclusions about him—when I shouldn't have. Nor should I have let old fears and insecurities creep to the surface. Liam is not like the other men in my life. Not one little bit, and now I'm afraid he's never going to talk to me again.

"Penny for your thoughts." I glance up and see Nina coming my way, Brandon and Casey at her side.

"Brandon. Casey," Gavin says and jumps up.

"What...what are you doing here?" I ask, my voice bordering on panic. Is she here to tell me off for selling a sex video and hurting her friend?

"I thought you might like to go for ice cream."

"Can we, Mom, can we?" Gavin asks, and I don't have the heart to say no.

"Sure, that would be nice," I say.

Nina glances around. "Can you get away?"

I snort, and shake my head. "I have all the time in the world. I was just fired."

Nina's face falls. She leans in and hugs me. "I'm so sorry, but you don't need this place. Not anymore."

God, she is so wrong about that. Everyone might think I made bank with the video, but they'd be wrong, and my bank has the barest of savings, especially after treating Liam to a night at the cabin.

"I just need a second." I struggle really hard to keep myself together and my tears at bay as I head to the back room and gather my things. I swallow hard, swat away the water leaking from my eyes, and plaster on a smile as I meet Nina and the boys.

"All set?" she asks.

I nod, and we head outside. The sun falls over us, but it does little to warm the chill in my bones. I glance around. "Walk or drive?" I ask.

"I'll drive," Nina says, and I'm grateful for that. I don't have the concentration and will likely wrap old Dixey around a lamp pole.

We all climb into her SUV, and I turn to find her staring at me. Liam is her friend, not mine, and she'll always take his side, but she's here with me now, so that counts for something. Can I open up to her? "Nina."

"Yeah?"

I bite the inside of my cheek hard enough to cause pain. "I think I made a big mistake."

She gives me a smile, reaches across the seat and gives my hand a squeeze. "You really love him, huh?"

I nod, and try so hard not to cry. I don't want to upset Gavin, Brandon or Casey, and I'm so grateful that Nina still wants them to be friends. "I think you two need to talk." She starts the vehicle, and pulls into traffic.

I shake my head as I stare at the road through watery eyes. "I don't think he'll ever talk to me again."

"Why is that?"

"Because he thinks I sold the video of us. It's not the first time something like this happened to him, some girl betrayed him."

"Yeah, but you're not 'any' girl." I stare at her, and she gives me a soft smile. "What made you fall in love with him?"

I laugh and curl my fingers around my purse as I consider our last month together. "It's crazy."

"Tell me."

"He presents this big loud, rough and rebellious image to the world, but underneath that, he's just the sweetest guy. Quiet, a little introverted."

"Just a little?" she says, like she understands exactly what I'm saying.

"Okay, maybe a lot."

"That must be exhausting."

"Yeah, I think it takes its toll on him." I glance over my shoulder. "He's so good with Gavin. He's real, you know. He sees the best in him, and is so patient." I glance ahead and have no idea what ice cream store she's taking us to, but we're pretty close to my neighborhood.

"So, you think a guy like that would just think the worst of you?"

"I..." I look down, my thoughts jumbled.

"Did you think the worst when Jeremy showed you the pictures of him and that girl?"

"No, I believed in him."

"Then why don't you think he believed in you too? The guy you just described to me." She shrugs. "I'm not so sure he's the kind of guy who'd just quit on the girl he loves."

"You...you think he loves me?"

She pulls up to the sidewalk, and I look around at the neighborhood, but don't see any ice cream shop. "Why don't you go find out," she says.

"What's...what's going on?"

"The boys and I are going for ice cream. We'll bring you back one. Now get out."

I stare at her, but she has a grin on her face. "And go where?"

She points to a house that looks like it's under construction. "In there. Now go. We need ice cream, and we need it now."

She practically kicks me from the vehicle and I slowly walk toward the house, glancing over my shoulder, trying to figure out what the hell is going on. Hammers pound, and men's voices reach my ears when I open the front door and peak in to find the place completely redone into what looks like a business of sorts.

Cole comes out from the back and goes still. "Oh hey," he says and checks his watch like he was expecting me.

"What's going on. What are you doing here?"

"Is she here yet?" I hear Violet scream out as she rounds the corner, wood chips in her hair and a hammer in her hand.

"What...the hell?"

"Oh hey," she says, a grin on her face.

"I thought you said you were busy today."

"Do I not look busy?" she counters, and I briefly close my eyes, sure I'm hallucinating. I open them again, only to find more people standing there staring at me. All Liam's family that I met at the Sunday barbecue, all the guys and wives I met at the rink, and Nina's barbecue party, and my small group of best friends.

"Somebody tell me what is going on."

Violet points behind me, and I spin so fast I nearly fall. The second I come face to face with Liam, dressed in a suit—and does he ever clean up nicely—I nearly sink to my knees, but for different reasons this time.

"Liam," I gasp, and I gaze the long length of him, noting the open wounds on his knuckles.

He glances past my shoulders. "If you could all give us a minute."

Shuffling sounds reach my ears as everyone clears out. "What's going on here?" I ask through a tight throat.

"This place is for you. Everyone has been helping me turn this place into a store, and a grooming station." He pauses and gestures to a small room. "That will be your office and maybe someday you can hang your veterinary license in there."

I shake my head, incredulous. He did this for me? "Liam, no, I can't. This is too much. I never wanted you to think...I was never using you for anything."

"I know." He takes three big steps and closes the distance between us and when he stands close, his presence overwhelming me, a flood of emotions squeezes my chest and there is nothing I can do to stop the tears.

"Hey," he says softly, and wipes my tears away. He touches my chin and lifts it until our eyes meet. "I've missed you."

"I didn't...didn't...wasn't responsible."

"I know you weren't. No matter how much Jeremy tried to convince me." He puts his hands over his heart. "I knew in here you had nothing to do with the video, which is why I made a visit to Devon Griffin's work."

My eyes widen, and my stomach turns. "What?"

He rubs his hand over my cheek. "You should have told me he stopped in at my place to see you, just like I should have told you he made a point of meeting me at Nelly's bar. At the time, he introduced himself as Griff, and I didn't put two and two together."

"I never told you his last name. I should have..." I take one of his hands, and lightly touch his sores. "You...you."

"We had a talk. With my fists. He won't ever hurt you again, Harper. My lawyer is involved now, too."

I shake my head. "I can't believe he...you...I can't believe any of this."

"The real question is, can you believe in me...?"

I gulp. "Liam, I never thought you were cheating. I wanted to talk to you. But Jeremy didn't want me around. He told me you were using me, and I mean, I know we weren't a couple, and we were playing house, and things weren't real..."

Stop rambling.

"That's where you're wrong, Harper. Things were very real for me, and Jeremy has been fired."

"Things...were real for me too." Another thought hits. "Jeremy told me you would lose your endorsements if there was any more bad publicity." I take a step back. "You shouldn't have gone after Devon...not for me. I don't want to be the one responsible—"

He captures my hand and pulls it back. "The only thing I care about are you and Gavin, and keeping you safe, and making you both mine. The endorsements don't matter."

"Making us both what?"

He drops to one knee and I gasp. "I love you, Harper. I swear I fell for you the second I set eyes on you."

I cry, hard. Oh my God, is this really happening? "You were everything I never expected, and there was no way I couldn't fall for you, Liam. That's on you."

He laughs, and the light, happy sound goes through me. He pulls out a velvet box and opens it. "Will you be my wife, Harper?"

I stare at the incredible kind and sensitive man I'm in love with, a man who trusted me enough to show me who he really was inside, and my heart fills with love.

"There is something you need to know before I answer."

His face falls, worry lines crinkling his dark eyes. "What?"

I smile, and drop to my knees with him. "You're my favorite. You were always my favorite."

He lets loose a bark of laughter and kisses me, and from behind I hear giggles, but I don't care who's watching. I'm so grateful to have this man, his family, his friends and mine all here to watch this. I just wish Gavin, Nina, Brandon and Casey were here too, but then I hear Gavin's voice and I look over my shoulder to see him and Holden licking ice creams and watching with wide eyes. Could my life be any more perfect than it is right now?

"That's a yes."

"I come with a son."

"I want your son, I want to adopt him. I want everything with you. Answer me, Harper. I'm a dying man right now."

I grin. "I can't really take all this. I need to work for it."

"Oh, you'll be working for it," he teases with a wink, and I laugh. "Besides, you can't say no. It's an engagement gift, so I need you to say—"

"Yes!" I yell, and he cups my cheek and gives me a kiss so steeped in love and promise, all I can do is cry.

"Is Liam going to be my daddy?" Gavin says.

"Yes, Gavin, he is," I say to him, then turn back to Liam.

He slides the gorgeous diamond onto my finger.

"But first," I say, lowering my voice for his ears only. "I'm taking you home, because right now, Liam, I need you to be my big daddy!"

Thank You!

Thank you so much for reading **The Rule Breaker**, book one in my Players on Ice series. I hope you enjoyed the story as much as I loved writing it. Please read on for an excerpt of **Single Dad Next Door.**

Interested in leaving a review? Please do! Reviews help readers connect with books that work for them. I appreciate all reviews, whether positive or negative.

Happy Reading,

Cathryn

SINGLE DAD NEXT DOOR

Rachel

When my bedroom door flies open and crashes hard against the paint-chipped wall, I groan. "Go away," I say, my voice muffled by my pillow. Not that my roommates will listen, even if they can hear me. Heck, I could scream at the top of my lungs and it wouldn't faze them, much less send them running back to their rooms —not when the view outside my window is that *hot*.

Seriously though, sharing a house with four college freshmen is not my idea of a good time, not when I'm a senior and working my ass off to get into law school. But when I left NYU two months before the start of my fourth year and transferred to Penn State at the last minute, this place was all I could find—and afford. Ultimately, Penn State is where I want to do my law degree after undergrad. I just ended up here sooner, rather than later.

Someone tugs at my pillow and I open one eye to see Becca hovering over me. "Come on, Rach, he just took his shirt off," she says. "You're going to want to see this."

Why oh why did my room have to come with the best view of the hot neighbor's driveway?

"Thank God for this heat wave." Sylvie, roommate number two, fans her face with her hand.

I groan and curl up into the fetal position. I just want one more minute in bed without every member of the house in my room. "I. Don't. Care." Well, that might be a lie. I like looking at the eye candy next door as well as they do, but after putting in a late night at Pizza Villa—I seriously have to find a new job—I need all the sleep I can get before class.

"Jesus, would you look at him," Becca says, her voice a breathy whisper as she peers out the window. "Talk about slurpalicious. I could seriously lick that from head to toe, and back up again."

"Leave," I say on a yawn.

Ignoring me, Sylvie squeals. "He's going back into his garage. Damned if he doesn't look as good going as he does coming."

"But I'd rather see him...*coming*," Becca says, and they start giggling.

"Seriously. Are you both twelve?"

"Shh, he's back," Becca says and swats her hand at me, like I'm an annoying fly that needs to be shooed away.

I shift on my bed, not to get a better look outside my window. No, moving has absolutely nothing at all to do with the shirtless mechanic turning my roommates into dim-witted moths. The *only* reason I'm getting up is to herd these girls from my room, and if I happen to get a glimpse of the hot, tattooed, badass daddy next door, well...then so be it.

I rub the blur from my eyes and toss my pillow at them. "Get away from my window, before he thinks it's me." They don't need to know that the hottie's bedroom window is also across from mine, and that late one night, he caught me staring into his room as he walked around in nothing but boxer shorts. Heck, if they knew that, they'd camp out for the rest of the school year, and that was so not happening.

"Ohmigod!" Sylvie leaps back. "I think he just saw me." She puts her hand over her mouth and starts to giggle. Footsteps pound down the hall, announcing the arrival of my other two roommates. I shake my head as they come bursting in.

Kill. Me. Now.

"Is he out there?" Val asks, her big blue eyes wide and hopeful.

"Yeah, but he saw me looking," Sylvie says. Despite that, she edges back around to sneak another look. Megan hurries across the room, and goes up on her toes to peer over Sylvie's shoulder, trying to catch a glimpse without getting caught.

"Do you really think he killed someone?" Megan asks.

"That's the rumor," Val protests, though her tone holds uncertain convictions.

"Then why isn't he in jail?"

"Maybe it was self-defense."

"He's such a badass."

"He's good with his little girl, though."

"Bad Boy Daddy, now that's hot."

"Do you think he'd spank me if I was bad?"

Unable to put up with their incessant chatter and giggles any longer, I point my finger toward the door. "Out. Now."

A chorus of grumbles ensues as they all sullenly walk to my door. Christ, I'm getting that lock fixed, even if I have to eat ramen noodles for the next month.

"God, you're such a grouch in the morning." Becca shoots me a wounded look over her shoulder.

"Doesn't even have to be the morning," Val adds with a hair toss.

"You need to get your nose out of a book once in a while," Megan says.

"What she needs is to get laid," Sylvie informs them all, but her solution to pretty much everything is sex. Problem is, this time Megan is nodding her head in sad agreement as she follows Sylvie out the door.

"I can hear you," I shout after them. I shake my head and my mussed hair falls over my shoulders. "I'm still right here." As I stand there, dressed only in my tank top and underwear, a warm breeze blows in and slides over my skin, a late reminder that I'd opened my window last night before crawling into bed exhausted. Great. Not only could the hot guy working on his car see my roommates drooling over him, he could *hear* them as well. *And* they just announced that I needed to get laid. How freaking mortifying. I stomp across the room and yell down the hall, "And don't bother to close my door on your way out." As usual my sarcasm is ignored.

I give the door a good slam, which helps improve my mood a little. With a deep breath, I turn around, not to see my hot neighbor, but to close my window. No way do I want him hearing anything else that goes on inside this place, or get the wrong idea that I might want him. I don't. Not in a million years.

I'm completely off guys, trying to keep a low profile. After my ex-boyfriend turned violent and abusive, threatening to kill me if I went to the police, I snuck away under the cover of darkness and put several states between us. He was big and hard like my neighbor, his muscles born from rough carpentry work. Last year, when he came to do repairs on the house I was sharing with friends, I was flattered that I was the object of his attention. At first he was doting and attentive, but as time went by, he became possessive and controlling. I came to find out later, he'd had other charges against him from numerous other women.

Jesus, why am I such a bad judge of character when it comes to men. Oh, probably because my only role model had been a mean-assed, alcoholic father who drove my beautiful, caring mom to an early grave and me out of the house the second I turned eighteen.

If I try hard enough I can still smell the cheap perfume on his shirt when he stumbled in after a weekend-long drinking binge. God, how I hated those women he slept around with almost as much as I hated my Dad. Mom used to try to protect me from his disgusting behavior, but what hurt the most was how he dragged Mom down, aging her pretty face far too early.

My heart squeezes as I think about her. She was a good woman, but was too afraid to leave. Running is hard. I get that now. Not that she really had anywhere to run. Our only other relative was my father's mother. She's still alive, living in upstate Pennsylvania where my Dad was born. While she liked me well enough, when it came to Mom and Dad, she always took Dad's side. That's how it is with parents, I guess.

I lift my arms, place my hands on the frame, and lean in to give it a tug when the hottie slowly lifts his head. Our eyes meet, hold a moment too long, and I suck in a quick breath as heat zings through me—and dammit, it's not the autumn sun that has warmth pooling between my legs.

OMFG.

With a wrench clasped tightly in his right hand he stares at me, like we're in a goddamn Mexican standoff. I swallow hard, and will myself to move, but can't seem to tear my gaze away. Ah, what was that I said about dim-witted moths?

Close the window, Rachel.

While my brain struggles to call the shots, my body has other ideas. Ideas that involve staying exactly where I am and ogling the hottest guy I'd ever seen. Blue eyes, square jaw, a body I could play Plinko on, and low riding, well-worn jeans that accentuate bulges in all the right places, and holy hell, the man has a lot of right places. Want prowls through me, hitting every erogenous spot along the way.

Just shut the window already.

He shifts his stance and taps the wrench against his leg as he looks up at me. A small grin touches his mouth, and that's when I realize I'm half naked. *Please, ground, open up and swallow me.* After hearing the girls, he probably thinks I'm trying to lure him to my room, fix that dry spell I've been going through. I grip the window ledge tighter and slam it down, putting the brakes on my body's reaction, and shutting out six delicious feet of hard muscle and pure testosterone.

This is so not what I need right now. Coffee. Yeah, that's what I need. Lots and lots of coffee.

I hurry to the kitchen and shove a pod into the Keurig. I pour milk into a cup and set it on the spill tray. As I wait for the coffee to percolate, I wander into the main level bathroom and glance in the mirror. I look at myself and try to imagine how I appeared through the blue-eyed mechanic's eyes. I see black smudges under tired eyes, boobs that only look big because I'm slender from work, school and lack of proper nutrition and rest. My hair is...wait... I grab a fistful of my curls and examine them closer. Oh, God, pizza sauce.

Could this day get any worse?

Christ, even if he did hear my roommates, I'm sure he'd never look twice at a girl like me—especially the way I look now. A guy like him probably goes out with women who are a little more put together, sexier. Although I have to say in the two months I've lived here, I've never seen a woman come or go from his place. Still, I'm certain a girl next door who always smells like marinara sauce and pepperoni isn't even on his radar.

Good, because I don't want to be.

The coffee machine beeps and I hurry back to the kitchen. I grab the mug to take a big sip. Heavenly. Desperate for a shower, to wash last night's work from my hair, I hurry back upstairs to my room, hot mug of coffee in hand. I check the time and grab my clothes. Giggles come from Sylvie's room across the hall as I dash into the bathroom. I turn the shower to cool, partly because it's just so hot in the house, and partly because I need to calm my overheated body down. I might be off men, especially big, scary ones like my neighbor, but my body and brain aren't working in sync this morning. Clearly my libido didn't get the memo when I left New York.

I stay under the needle-like spray longer than normal, needing an extra minute to clear my head. When the water turns cooler, I jump out, dry off, and pull on a pair of shorts and T-shirt. I towel dry my hair, then tie it back into a ponytail. I forgo makeup. Not only will it melt off my face, I'm not trying to impress anyone or draw any kind of attention to myself. Once done, I grab my purse, shove my textbooks into my backpack, and head for the front door, feeling a little more alive after the coffee.

The hot morning air hits like a slap in the face and I groan. It's October for God's sake. It's supposed to be time for pumpkin spiced lattes. This is more like beach weather. Mother nature needs to get her shit together. I glance at my watch, and judging by the time—thanks to an extra-long shower—I need to get my shit together, too. This morning I'll have to take my car to school, or risk being late for class. The walk to campus is long, around forty-five minutes, but I prefer it on days like today. I need to save my gas money for the colder winter months.

Since my driveway runs parallel to my neighbor's, I keep my head down, toss my backpack into the back seat and climb into the driver's side. Thank God the hottie is out of sight and I don't have to go through the embarrassment of facing him.

I roll my window down and shove the key into the ignition. I turn it, only for the engine to make some god-awful sound and stall out. My heart races quicker. Shit. Shit. Shit. Frustrated, I give the steering wheel a thump with my fist. This can't be happening. I need this car. Need to be able to depend on it if I have to run again. It might be an old junker, but it's all I have. I can't afford a new one. Heck, I'm on such a tight budget, I can't even afford to have this one fixed.

I take a deep breath, throw up a silent prayer, and twist the key again, only for it to cough and gasp, like it's dying a slow and painful death.

No. No. No

A tap comes on the roof, and I turn to see my hot—shirtless—neighbor with his arms braced over the door of my car. He leans down, his beautiful face close to mine. "Need a hand?"

"I...uh...it's not working."

Jeez, way to state the obvious.

He grins, and when I see a cute dimple that contrasts sharply with his chiseled face, I nearly swallow my tongue.

"Yeah, I kind of got that, you know, being a mechanic and all." As he gives off a bad-boy vibe that messes with my common sense, he grabs a cloth from his back pocket, and wipes his hands before leaning into the car, his head practically in my lap.

Holy fuck!

It takes everything, and I mean *everything*, in me not to grab the back of his head and shove it between my legs. My sex practically quivers at the visual. The girls were right. I do need to get laid. I bite the inside of my cheek to stifle the moan rising in my throat.

"What...what are you doing?" I finally manage to ask, and will myself not to writhe restlessly, and show him what a needy girl I really am.

He pulls the hood release, and the front end of my car jumps. His head lifts and once again his face is close to mine. "Popping the hood." He angles his head, and his eyes narrow. "What did you think I was doing?"

Oh, I don't know. Maybe you were taking this opportunity to go down on me.

"Popping the hood," I say quickly, and try not to think of sex. Dirty sex. Take-me-up-against-the-wall kind of sex. Not that I know anything about that. Sadly.

His laugh is rough and deep as he walks around to the front of the car, and I unbuckle quickly. My legs wobble as I climb out of the driver's seat and follow him. He's grinning when I reach him.

"What?" I ask, my voice raspy.

He touches my cracked windshield washer cap, which I happened to repair all by myself. "Duct tape?" he asks, his voice amused.

"Tools of the trade, right," I say and try not to sound as breathless as I feel. A difficult task considering I'm standing next to a half-naked man that I want to run my hands all over. I mean I've seen shirtless guys before, but come on. This guy is like a freaking viking. He leans forward to fiddle with something, and the movement shows off impressive bicep muscles. I break a sweat as his closeness sends shudders of need between my thighs. Honest to God, the man is a work of art, and all I can think of is no-strings sex—something I've never done before. But that's crazy and reckless and so not me. Truthfully, if I knew what was good for me, I'd slam the hood shut and run in the opposite direction.

I'm about to do just that when he says, "Uh, huh."

"Is...is there something wrong?" Is that my voice? Christ, I sound like I'm whacked out on painkillers.

For God's sake, get it together, girl.

He rubs the scruff on his chin, and I step back, needing a measure of distance before I actually reach out and run my hands over all his hard grooves and deep valleys.

"Plenty," he says again and checks something else. I have no clue what he's doing. I only know that he looks as hot as hell doing it. As he leans over my car, my gaze slides to his ass, committing the way his pants cup his cheeks to memory. The guy could be in a jeans commercial, or better yet, a Calvin Klein underwear ad. I'm a girl, but advertising like that would have me one-clicking the buy button.

My heart hammers as he stands again. He turns toward me, but I'm far too slow to react. His eyes are piercing, almost a deeper shade of blue when my gaze jerks to his, and I can't tell whether he's thrilled or pissed to find me checking him out.

I step closer and look over the engine. "So, what is it?" I ask, disgusted with myself. I should not be fantasizing over this man.

He clears his throat. "I think the first thing we need to do is replace the spark plugs," he answers, his voice a little hoarse.

"Yeah, that's what I was thinking," I say, my head bobbing in agreement.

That grin is back when I look at him. "You know something about cars?"

I shrug. "Sure...and duck tape."

He laughs and says, "It's not..." he shakes his head. "Never mind. So, you agree then, that something's not firing right?"

Firing? Oh, things were firing all right, and lighting up my body like a goddamn Fourth of July celebration.

Damn him.

Damn Mother Nature.

Damn dim-witted moths.

His Strings to Pull

His Trouble in Talulah

His Taste of Temptation

His Moment to Steal

His Best Friend's Girl

His Reason to Stay

Confessions

Confessions of a Bad Boy Professor

Confessions of a Bad Boy Officer

Confessions of a Bad Boy Fighter

Confessions of a Bad Boy Gamer

Confessions of a Bad Boy Millionaire

Confessions of a Bad Boy Santa

Confessions of a Bad Boy CEO

Hands On

Hands On

Body Contact

Full Exposure

Dossier

Private Reserve

House Rules

Under Pressure

Big Catch

Brazilian Fantasy

Improper Proposal

Boys of Beachville

Good at Being Bad

Igniting the Bad Boy

Bad Girl Therapy

Stone Cliff Series:

Crashing Down

Wasted Summer

Love Lessons

Wrapped Up

Eternal Pleasure Series

Instinctive

Impulsive

Indulgent

Sun Stroked Series

Seaside Seduction

Deep Desire

Private Pleasure

Captured and Claimed Series:

Yours to Take

Yours to Teach

Yours to Keep

Firefighter Heat Series

Fever

Siren

Flash Fire

Playing For Keeps Series

Slow Ride

Wild Ride

Sweet Ride

Breaking the Rules:

Hold Me Down Hard

Pin Me Up Proper

Tie Me Down Tight

Stand Alone Title:

Hands on with the CEO

Torn Between Two Brothers

Holiday Spirit

Unleashed

Knocking on Demon's Door

Web of Desire

Pinterest http://www.pinterest.com/catkalen/